閱讀可以輕鬆學！

理解文章 × 活用文法 × 連接上下文

讓閱讀可以直覺反應

讀英文長文不再卡卡的！

　　在我個人過去多年的教學經驗和學習經驗，發現英文閱讀一直是諸多英語學習者難以駕馭的範圍。總是會聽到很多學生有這些問題：「為什麼已經讀了很多遍，還是理解錯」、「每個單字都知道意思，但是放進文章中又沒讀懂」、「閱讀總是花費最多時間，怎麼樣才可以迅速讀完一篇文章呢？」其實會有這些難題是因為英文閱讀是全方面的在運用英文，不僅牽涉到字彙量，與對片語的熟用能力以及文句的理解都有密切的關係。

　　在各大英文考試中，都能看見閱讀的身影，閱讀測驗總是被安排在最後一個大題，不僅考的是對英文的融會貫通，更是考驗考生對時間的掌控，可見閱讀對於英文的重要。因此本書從考試常見 3 大題型，深入剖析 31 個主題的文章，讓讀者可以學習如何正確運用單字、活用片語、理解句子銜接關係。每道測驗題搭配中文翻譯，提示出關鍵單字，在閱讀每篇文章的同時可以一邊增加字彙量，一邊熟悉考試可能出現的各種題型，不僅打穩考試實力，也同步提升閱讀能力，更能全方位增強英文實力！

閱讀是相當重要的技能，只要學習英文，無處不需要它，並且閱讀理解的能力可以看出一個人的語言基礎是否扎實、能否活用所學。但是培養閱讀能力不是一朝一夕能夠達成的，也沒有一步登天的方法，只要每天持續練習，養成閱讀的好習慣，藉由一篇篇的短文，逐步累積自己的閱讀實力和英文能力，相信在職場或是國際觀的提升上絕對有莫大的助益。

　　希望本書能減少讀者對閱讀的恐懼，透過書中各種主題的文章與習題，學會抓住閱讀的重點句子及關鍵字，破解閱讀文章的結構，讓大家不再害怕長文，只要多練習閱讀題型，一定能使閱讀能力大幅提升！本書也期望讓各位在學習英文的路上，用輕鬆喜悅的心情邁進。提升閱讀能力，英語實力才會好！

使用說明

閱讀並不困難

掌握閱讀測驗解題技巧,輕鬆理解文章、拿高分!

1. 用英文腦理解文章

和中文不同,英文文章的結構多為破題法,第一段就可以看出文章重點,之後再補充敘述。因此要戰勝落落長的英文文章,只要分割文章結構,就能找出重點訊息!

Unit 01 Traffic Safety
交通安全篇

Unit 01-1: 文章概要及重點理解
閱讀全文,並回答下列的問題

Drunk driving has become a serious form of murder. Every day about twenty-six Americans on the average are killed by drunk drivers. Although, heavy drinking used to be an acceptable part of the American masculine image, drunken killers have recently caused so many tragedies that the public is no longer tolerant.

Twenty states in the United States have raised the legal drinking age to 21, reversing a trend of 1960s to reduce it to 18. After New Jersey lowered it to 18, the number of people killed by 18-to-20-year-old drivers doubled, so the state recently upped it back to 21. Some states are also punishing bars for serving customers too many drinks. What's more, as accidents continue to occur daily, some Americans are even beginning to suggest a national prohibition of alcohol. Reformers, however, think that legal prohibition and raising the drinking age will have little effect unless accompanied by educational programs to help young people develop responsible attitudes about drinking.

008

Unit 02 Humanities Issues
人文議題篇

Unit 02-1: 文章概要及重點理解
閱讀全文,並回答下列的問題

The Seven Wonders of the Ancient World is a list of seven manmade structures that have been objects of wonder throughout history, objects that amaze and astonish those who see them. While a number of lists of ancient wonders have been proposed, the one universally agreed on is the one consisting of the Great Pyramid of Giza, the Hanging Gardens of Babylon, the Temple of Artemis, the Statue of Zeus, the Lighthouse of Alexandria, the Colossus of Rhodes, and the Mausoleum of Maussollos. Due to the fact that the original list was created by the Greeks, the wonders chosen were mostly Greek, or at least from cultures that the Greeks were familiar with. It is thus not surprising that the Great Wall of China and Stonehenge of England are not on the list. Left at the mercy of time and warring civilizations, six of these wonders have been destroyed, and only the Great Pyramid has survived to the present day. Each is a monument to the amazing problem-solving skills of the ancient people who, in a time before modern construction technology, managed to undertake projects that have continued to excite people's

016

2. 掌握前後文

在中文裡，遇到不懂的字，文章還是有辦法讀懂，英文也一樣！
單字背得再多、句型學得再深，一定還是會有看不懂的字，因此
不要被不懂的地方卡住了，掌握前後文也能看懂英文文章，破解
克漏字、前後文句子等閱讀難題！

3. 熟用英文片語、慣用語

在寫作文時，我們會常引用俗語、成語在在文章中，英文文章也是
一樣，很常會運用片語和慣用語，如果不懂片語和慣用語的涵義，
就可能因誤解文意而看不懂文章。因此熟悉片語、慣用語對於閱讀
的理解，是相當重要的一環！每單元補充關鍵單字和片語，輕鬆理
解文章！

增強閱讀能力的 3 個習慣

許多心理學家提倡「21 天效應」，指一件事保持 21 天就能養成習慣。想要增強閱讀能力並非一朝一夕，養成 3 個習慣，閱讀理解就能日益增長！

1. 保持閱讀習慣

閱讀能力的提升不能一步登天，得穩紮穩打。首先確定自己的閱讀程度，並選擇適合且有興趣的文章，每天撥出一點點時間閱讀，第一周看 3 行、第二周 4 行、第三周 5 行……，到最後對英文的理解力和閱讀速度必會日益增強。

2. 養成記錄習慣

在閱讀文章時，一定會出現一些你看不懂的字，先別急著查！記錄下來，透過上下文知道大概的故事內容，推測單字和文章意思。在閱讀完文章後，再將那些猜測的單字整理出來，製作出一本屬於你自己的單字書，就能針對自己不懂的單字複習，讓單字更加深刻的記憶在腦中。

3. 培養複習習慣

讀一篇文章時一定有很多不懂的字、句型和用法，因此在查詢完意思之後，再閱讀一次，能聚焦這些不懂的地方，加深留存在腦海的印象。

★本書之前：踏出閱讀的第一步

很多人單字量多、文法不錯，但還是會卡在閱讀；許多人看到篇幅較長的英文文章，就亂了陣腳，想讀得快卻越讀越不懂。其實閱讀的關鍵在於理解含意，並活用單字、片語、文法和句型，閱讀要好，全方位的能力不能少。如果看到長篇文章會害怕，試試短文吧！一段一段地讀懂，掌握關鍵的單字和句子，就能輕鬆看懂英文文章，讓自己的閱讀能力大幅提升！

掌握關鍵字輕鬆讀文章

<u>Fiction</u> is the name we use for stories that are <u>make-believe</u>, such as *Harry Potter* or *Alice in the Wonderland*. But fiction isn't always different from the way things usually are.It can be so close to the truth that it seems as real as something that happened to you this morning. Or, fiction can be as <u>fantastic</u> as the most unbelievable <u>fairy tale</u>.

★ 文章出自 p.20

關鍵字

看到這些字就可以很清楚的知道這篇文章的重點了！

1. fiction 小說
2. make-believe 虛構的
3. *Harry Potter* or *Alice in the Wonderland*
   《哈利波特》和《愛麗絲夢遊仙境》
4. fantastic 夢幻的
5. fairy tale 童話故事

中文翻譯

我們稱那些虛構的故事，像是《哈利波特》和《愛麗絲夢遊仙境》等為小說。但小說並不總是和事情原本的樣子不同。它可以如此貼近現實，就像今天早晨發生在身上的事情一樣真實。小說也可以像最難以相信的童話故事一般夢幻。

掌握關鍵字輕鬆讀文章

Known as <u>Sakura</u> in Japanese, these trees actually have <u>powerful ties</u> to the country's history and culture. Cherry blossoms are considered the embodiment of <u>Wabi-Sab philosophy</u>. It is <u>an attitude of accepting the imperfectness</u> of life in ancient Japanese aesthetic ideas.

★ 文章出自 p.28

關鍵字

看到這些字就可以很清楚的知道這篇文章的重點了！

1. Sakura 櫻花
2. powerful ties 很深的淵源
3. Wabi-Sab philosophy 日本哲學「侘寂」
4. an attitude of accepting the imperfectness 接受不完美的態度

中文翻譯

櫻花在日文中叫做「Sakura」，而櫻花樹其實和該國的歷史及文化有很深的淵源。櫻花被視為是一種日本哲學「侘寂」的體現。它代表一種古老日本美學，是接受生命不完美的態度。

掌握關鍵字輕鬆讀文章

Melbourne's <u>climate</u> is excitingly <u>variable</u>, with warm to hot dry summers and cool, crisp, wet winters. <u>Magnificent</u> autumns and springs provide spectacular scenes of changing leaves and <u>blossoms</u>.

★ 文章出自 p.72

關鍵字

看到這些字就可以很清楚的知道這篇文章的重點了！

1. climate 氣候
2. variable 多變的
3. magnificent 華麗的
4. blossoms 花朵

中文翻譯

墨爾本的氣候多變頗令人興奮，從溫暖和乾熱的夏天到寒冷、刺骨又潮溼的冬天都有。怡人的春秋兩季帶來百花綻放的壯觀景色。

掌握關鍵字輕鬆讀文章

In Taiwan, <u>typhoons</u> usually come in summer. They bring <u>strong wind</u> and lots of <u>rainfall</u>. The <u>weather bureau</u> will warn us one or two days before they come. You can see people <u>doing such things as</u> cutting down tall trees and fixing their houses.

★ 文章出自 p.96

關鍵字

看到這些字就可以很清楚的知道這篇文章的重點了！

1. typhoon 颱風
2. strong wind 強風
3. rainfall 大雨
4. weather bureau 氣象局
5. doing such things as 做這一類的事

中文翻譯

颱風經常在夏天侵襲臺灣，帶來強風和豐沛的雨量。颱風來臨之前，氣象局會預先發佈颱風警報，這個時候，可以看到民眾進行砍大樹、維修房屋等防颱措施。

掌握關鍵字輕鬆讀文章

Do you ever wonder where all the money in your <u>wallet</u> goes? If you do, maybe it's time to examine your <u>spending habits</u>. Think about <u>purchases</u> before you make them. Ask yourself questions like these:

- Can I do without it?
- Can I continue to use what I already have?
- Can I substitute something less expensive?
- Is it <u>a want or a need</u>?
- Why do I want to buy it?

Learn to say "no" to <u>unnecessary</u> purchases. Then you'll have money to buy the things you really want or need.

★ 文章出自 p.42

關鍵字

看到這些字就可以很清楚的知道這篇文章的重點了！

1. wallet 錢包
2. spending habits 消費習慣
3. purchase 購買
4. a want or a need 想要還是需要
5. unnecessary 不必要的

中文翻譯

你曾懷疑錢包裡的錢都到哪裡去了嗎？如果有，也許是檢視花錢習慣的時候了。在出手購買前要三思，問自己這些問題：

- 沒有它行嗎？
- 可以繼續使用我原本有的東西嗎？
- 可以用比較便宜的東西取代嗎？
- 這是想要的東西還是需要的東西？
- 我為什麼想買它？

學習對非必要的東西說「不」，你就會有錢去購買真正想要或需要的東西了。

掌握關鍵字輕鬆讀文章

In addition to food and shelter, man has another important need. It is <u>clothing</u>. Man wears clothing for at least three <u>purposes</u>, namely, <u>for protection, for decoration, and for modesty</u>. In other words, clothing can protect us from the rain and from the sun. It can also make us look handsome or beautiful. Moreover, it can reflect the manners we have, and it shows our personal preferences toward clothing, for <u>fashion tastes</u> vary.

★ 文章出自 p.34

關鍵字

看到這些字就可以很清楚的知道這篇文章的重點了！

1. clothing 服裝
2. purpose 目的
3. for protection, for decoration, and for modesty
   為了保護、裝飾、表示莊重
4. fashion tastes 時尚品味

中文翻譯

在食物和居所之外，人有另一個重要的需求──服裝。人們穿衣服至少是為了這三個目的──保護、裝飾、表示莊重。換句話說，衣服可以保護我們不被日曬雨淋。也可以使我們看起來英俊或美麗。此外，服裝更可以反映我們的風度，並展出我們對於服裝的個人喜好，因為時尚品味是因人而異的。

掌握關鍵字輕鬆讀文章

The differences in language, custom, and religious beliefs in an <u>intercultural family</u> may bring about some challenges. However, kids in such family can actually <u>benefit from such background</u>. First, children can <u>spontaneously</u> learn to be <u>multi-lingual</u> in the early stage of development. Also, they could learn to be more <u>tolerant</u> to different religious beliefs and practices. With positive attitude, the intercultural marriage can help the family to embark on a wonderful journey of discovery and happiness.

★ 文章出自 p.120

關鍵字

看到這些字就可以很清楚的知道這篇文章的重點了！

1. intercultural family 跨文化家庭
2. benefit from such background 從這種背景受益
3. spontaneously 自然地
4. multi-lingual 多種語言
5. tolerant 寬容的

中文翻譯

在跨文化家庭中，語言、習俗、以及宗教信仰上的差異可能會帶來一些挑戰。但是，這種家庭背景下其實對小孩有一些好處。首先，小孩可以在早期發展階段就自然地學習多種語言。此外，他們可以學習對不同的宗教信仰和行為模式抱持寬容的態度。有了正面的態度，跨文化婚姻可以幫助家庭開啟一段充滿新發現的幸福旅程。

掌握關鍵字輕鬆讀文章

Most of us spend a third of our lives <u>asleep</u>. Scientists have been studying the brain to learn <u>what happens while we sleep</u>. Scientists tell us that there are <u>four stages of sleep</u>. During each stage our brain behaves differently, and so does our body. Each stage is marked by changes in the pattern of <u>brain waves</u>, which can <u>be recorded by machine</u>.

★ 文章出自 p.168

關鍵字
看到這些字就可以很清楚的知道這篇文章的重點了！
1. asleep 睡著
2. what happens while we sleep 睡眠時發生什麼事
3. four stages of sleep 睡眠 4 階段
4. brain waves 腦波
5. be recorded by machine 被機器記錄

中文翻譯
大多數的人把生命的三分之一花在睡眠上。為了瞭解人在睡眠時會發生什麼事，科學家一直在研究人腦。科學家表示，睡眠有四個階段。在每個階段當中，我們的頭腦會有不同的表現，我們的身體亦然。每個階段是以腦波型態的變化為其特徵，而腦波是可以用機器記錄下來的。

9

掌握關鍵字輕鬆讀文章

<u>Cockroaches</u> seem very <u>adaptable</u>. Regardless of what kind of poison is set out for them, they seem to <u>adjust</u> very quickly to it. If they are somehow eliminated from one part of the house, they simply move to a different part. The war of human against roaches is likely to <u>continue for a long time to come</u>.

★ 文章出自 p.184

關鍵字

看到這些字就可以很清楚的知道這篇文章的重點了！

1. Cockroach 蟑螂
2. adaptable 適應性強
3. adjust 適應
4. continue for a long time to come 還會繼續下去

中文翻譯

蟑螂似乎適應力很強。不管人們放哪一種毒藥，牠們似乎很快就能適應。要是牠們莫名其妙地消失在房子的某部份，那麼一定是搬到另一個地方去了。人和蟑螂之間的戰爭很可能在未來還得繼續下去。

10

掌握關鍵字輕鬆讀文章

People talk about <u>love at first sight</u>. It happens, but <u>rarely</u>. Making a life-long <u>commitment</u> too soon can be <u>a recipe for disaster</u>. Give yourself time to really get to know the person first.

★ 文章出自 p.66

關鍵單字

看到這些單字就可以很清楚的知道這篇文章的重點了！

1. love at first sight 一見鍾情
2. rarely 稀少
3. commitment 承諾
4. a recipe for disaster 不幸的根源

中文翻譯

人們談到一見鍾情。這是可能發生的，但很少。過於倉促許下一生的承諾可能是不幸的根源。給自己時間先真正的去認識這個人吧！

掌握關鍵字輕鬆讀文章

Many <u>developed nations</u> are facing the issues of the <u>aging population</u>. To deal with <u>potential problems</u> of an aging society, the government of Taiwan has launched a <u>long-term care plan</u>. The Ministry of Health and Welfare (MOHW) has been promoting the National Ten-year Long-term Care Plan 2.0 since 2005. More people can have access to resources of the public long-term care system.

★ 文章出自 p.48

關鍵字

看到這些字就可以很清楚的知道這篇文章的重點了！

1. developed nation 已開發國家
2. aging population 人口老化
3. potential problem 潛在問題
4. aging society 高齡化社會
5. long-term care plan 長照計畫

中文翻譯

許多已開發國家都面臨到人口老化的問題。為了處理高齡化社會的潛在問題，臺灣的政府已經發起了長期照護計畫。衛生福利部從 2005 年開始就在推動國家十年長期照護 2.0 計畫。更多人可以用到公共長期照護系統的資源。

Contents 目錄

英文閱讀

3

大題型
完整攻克
秘笈

Unit 01 Traffic Safety
交通安全篇

Unit 01-1: 文章概要及重點理解
閱讀全文，並回答下列的問題

Drunk driving has become a serious form of murder. Every day about twenty-six Americans on the average are killed by drunk drivers. Although, heavy drinking used to be an acceptable part of the American masculine image, drunken killers have recently caused so many tragedies that the public is no longer tolerant.

Twenty states in the United States have raised the legal drinking age to 21, reversing a trend of 1960s to reduce it to 18. After New Jersey lowered it to 18, the number of people killed by 18-to-20-year-old drivers doubled, so the state recently upped it back to 21. Some states are also punishing bars for serving customers too many drinks. What's more, as accidents continue to occur daily, some Americans are even beginning to suggest a national prohibition of alcohol. Reformers, however, think that legal prohibition and raising the drinking age will have little effect unless accompanied by educational programs to help young people develop responsible attitudes about drinking.

( ) 1. **Drunk driving has become a major problem in America because _____.**
(A) most murderers are heavy drinkers
(B) many Americans drink too much
(C) most drivers are too young
(D) many traffic accidents are caused by heavy drinking

( ) 2. **What is the public opinion regarding heavy drinking?**
(A) It's a manly image.
(B) It can create a relaxing and happy atmosphere.
(C) Fewer and fewer people can stand it.
(D) People should be careful in choosing the right drink.

( ) 3. **According to reformers, the best way to solve the problem of drunk driving is to _____.**
(A) specify the amount drivers can drink
(B) couple education with legal measures
(C) forbid liquor drinking
(D) raise the drinking age

( ) 4. **What happened when New Jersey lowered the legal age of drinking to 18?**
(A) Nothing is changed.
(B) The number of people killed by 18-to-20-year-old drivers tripled.
(C) It didn't bring a positive effect.
(D) The legal drinking age was immediately changed it back to 21.

The automobile has introduced new **patterns**[01] of American social life. **Ownership**[02] of a car is ____1____ an economic necessity but a social one; as a matter of fact, ownership of two cars is rapidly coming ____2____, in middle-class families, a necessity. The car is the symbol of being ____3____ ; for the young, it is the symbol of **arriving at manhood**[03]. It is a ____4____ of **courtship**[04]; without it, the institution of marriage itself might collapse!

However, everything has two sides. A car can be a **stimulus**[05] for bad **temper**[06] and a school for bad manners. It also causes a rising number of crime: 600,000 automobile ____5____ are reported every year, ____6____ minor **offenses**[07] –speeding, illegal parking, etc., -are too numerous even ____7____ computer statistics. It is one of the major killers: it ____8____ a **toll**[08] of 55,000 lives every year and has claimed altogether, since its invention, over 2,000,000 lives – more than three ____9____ the total of all battle **casualties**[09] in all wars in which the United States has been engaged. ____10____, this machine of great convenience may also come as a **weapon**[10] of great danger. We all need to be careful.

單字片語補充站

01 **pattern** [名] 模式

02 **ownership** [名] 擁有、所有權

03 **arrive at manhood** [片] 成年

04 **stimulus** [名] 刺激

05 **courtship** [名] 求愛、追求

06 **temper** [名] 脾氣

07 **offense** [名] 違反

08 **toll** [名] 傷亡人數

09 **casualty** [名] 死傷人員

10 **weapon** [名] 武器

 Quiz

( ) **01.** (A) not　　(B) not only　　(C) not mere　　(D) not the same

( ) **02.** (A) to be　(B) to get　　(C) to do　　(D) to have

( ) **03.** (A) nothing　　　(B) someone else
(C) nobody　　　(D) somebody

( ) **04.** (A) weapon　　　(B) experiment
(C) communication　(D) medium

( ) **05.** (A) thefts　(B) murder　(C) disappearance　(D) killing

( ) **06.** (A) but　　(B) as　　(C) when　　(D) while

( ) **07.** (A) on　　(B) to　　(C) for　　(D) at

( ) **08.** (A) takes　(B) displays　(C) proves　(D) declare

( ) **09.** (A) times　(B) tides　(C) space　(D) size

( ) **10.** (A) In total　　　(B) In other words
(C) In short　　　(D) At length

There is no doubt that the phenomenon of **road rage**[01] exists. _____1_____ Road rage seems to be on the increase and this may be due to the following **factors**[02]. First, there are more cars competing for road space. _____2_____ For example, a person has to **meet a deadline**[03], but is caught in a **tangle**[04] of traffic. He or she then may feel increasingly **frustrated**[05]. _____3_____ Nowadays, a person may **be bombarded with**[06] more concerns and worries than before and **seem to**[07] forget how to be **polite**[08]. In this way, since cars are becoming a necessity, drivers should consider a plan of action against road rage. _____4_____ The drivers must know the **attack**[09] of road rage will not get them any farther but could only result in a serious health problem. The best way is to leave oneself more time in order not to rush. _____5_____ This could give the driver at least a twenty or thirty minutes **leeway**[10].

單字片語補充站

01 road rage
[片] 駕駛因壓力或他人駕駛行為表現出的憤怒或暴力行為

02 factor [名] 因素、原因

03 meet a deadline
[片] 在最後期限內完成某事

04 tangle [名] 糾結、紛亂

05 frustrated [形] 受挫的、沮喪

06 be bombarded with
[片] 被（事情）轟炸

07 seem to [片] 似乎

08 polite [形] 有禮貌的

09 attack [名] 攻擊

10 leeway [名] 時間等的餘地

 **Quiz**

(A) Another factor may be that people are not as courteous as they used to be.

(B) A change in mental attitude is the first step.

(C) People are far more subject to time constraints.

(D) In a recent survey, nine out of ten drivers admit to having felt intense anger toward other drivers at some time.

(E) One could leave home earlier or make better arrangement with one's schedule.

Unit 01-1: 文章概要及重點理解

酒醉駕車已經變成一種謀殺的形式。每天平均有大約二十六個美國人被酒醉駕駛者奪去性命。雖然酗酒過去曾經被視為是美國男性氣概的象徵，但酒醉駕駛者最近卻造成無數的悲劇以致於大眾已不再能接受這種行為。

美國有 20 個州現已提高法定喝酒年齡到 21 歲，與 1960 年代將它降低為 18 歲的趨勢完全相反。在紐澤西州將年齡降到 18 歲後，被18 歲到 20 歲右的駕駛者奪去性命的總人數竟然增加一倍，所以該州最近已將它又提高到 21 歲。有些州也下令懲罰酒吧提供顧客太多酒的情形。除此之外，隨著傷亡名單每日出現，有些美國人甚至開始建議全國性禁酒。然而，改革者認為法律禁止以及提高喝酒年紀只能產生一點點的效果，除非伴隨教育方面的計劃課程去幫助年輕人培養負責的飲酒態度。

(D) 1. 酒醉駕車已經變成一種重大的問題，因為：
　　　A. 大部分殺人犯都大量飲酒　　B. 許多美國人喝太多
　　　C. 大部分駕駛太年輕　　　　　**D. 很多交通意外皆由酒醉駕車引起。**

(C) 2. 大眾輿論如何看待酗酒？
　　　A. 很有男子氣概　　　　　　　B. 可以創造放鬆快樂的氣氛
　　　C. 愈來愈少的人能夠容忍了。　D. 人們應該謹慎選擇飲料

(B) 3. 根據改革者，最佳的解決酒醉駕車的方法是：
　　　A. 明確說明駕駛可以飲酒的份量　**B. 教育跟法律方面的措施互相配合。**
　　　C. 禁止飲用酒精飲料　　　　　　D. 提高法定飲酒年齡

(C) 4. 當紐澤西將法定飲酒年齡降至18時，發生了什麼事？
　　　A. 什麼都沒有改變。
　　　B. 因 18 至 20 歲駕駛者喪命的人數增了三倍。
　　　C. 它並未帶來正面的影響。
　　　D. 法定飲酒年齡立刻被改回 21 歲。

Unit **01-2:** 透過克漏字題型強化文法概念

汽車引進了美國社交生活新的模式。擁有一部汽車不僅在經濟上和社交上都不可或缺，事實上，中產階級家庭很快就變得需要擁有二部車子了。有部車子是「重要人物」的象徵，對年輕人而言，它就是長大成人的象徵。它也是追求異性的媒介物，沒有車子，婚姻制度可能崩潰！

然而，任何事物都是一體兩面的，車子會激起火爆的脾氣，也是不良行為的培育所，且造成犯罪率的上升。每年有 60 萬件汽車竊案的報導，輕微的犯法如超速、違規停車等等案件，數量太多以致於連電腦都無法統計。車子是主要的殺人兇手之一：它每年奪走了 5 萬 5 千條人命，從汽車的發明以來，據稱已奪走了 2 百萬條的人命，遠超過所有美國參予的戰爭的陣亡士兵生命的三倍。簡而言之，這個給人們生活中最大方便的機器，也可能是很危險的武器。我們都應謹慎小心。

1.B 2.A 3.D 4.D 5.A 6.D 7.C 8.A 9.A 10.C

Unit **01-3:** 熟悉篇章的前後銜接關係

毫無疑問地，道路憤怒的現象的確存在。**(D) 最近的調查發現，十分之九的駕駛承認有時候會對其他的駕駛感到憤怒。**道路憤怒似乎正逐漸增加，而這可能是因為下列因素。首先，有越來越多的汽車為道路空間競爭，**(C) 人們更加感受到時間限制。**例如，一個人必須趕時間，但是卻被困在混亂的交通裡，他或她就可能會更加感到挫折。**(A) 另一個因素可能是人們不如以前有禮貌。**現在的人和以前的人相較，可能被更多憂心的事困擾，而似乎忘了如何保持禮貌。這樣的話，既然汽車逐漸成為必需品，駕駛人就應該考慮計畫抵抗道路憤怒的行動。**(B) 改變內心的態度是第一步。**駕駛人必須知道道路憤怒的攻擊不但不會讓車子前進，還可能會導致嚴重的健康問題。最好的方式就是讓自己擁有更多時間，避免匆忙。**(E) 我們可以早點出門或做更好的時間安排。**這樣可以讓駕駛人至少有二十或三十分鐘緩衝空檔。

1.D 2.C 3.A 4.B 5.E

Unit 02-1: 文章概要及重點理解
閱讀全文，並回答下列的問題

The Seven Wonders of the Ancient World is a list of seven manmade structures that have been objects of wonder throughout history, objects that amaze and astonish those who see them. While a number of lists of ancient wonders have been proposed, the one universally agreed on is the one consisting of the Great Pyramid of Giza, the Hanging Gardens of Babylon, the Temple of Artemis, the Statue of Zeus, the Lighthouse of Alexandria, the Colossus of Rhodes, and the Mausoleum of Maussollos. Due to the fact that the original list was created by the Greeks, the wonders chosen were mostly Greek, or at least from cultures that the Greeks were familiar with. It is thus not surprising that the Great Wall of China and Stonehenge of England are not on the list. Left at the mercy of time and warring civilizations, six of these wonders have been destroyed, and only the Great Pyramid has survived to the present day. Each is a monument to the amazing problem-solving skills of the ancient people who, in a time before modern construction technology, managed to undertake projects that have continued to excite people's imagination for centuries. Today, people still look to the ancient wonders for inspiration, so who knows how many of today's wonders were inspired by these ancient structures?

Quiz

( ) 1. **What information is NOT provided in the paragraph?**
  (A) Why the Seven Wonders have remained a source of inspiration.
  (B) The reason six out of the seven ancient wonders no longer exist.
  (C) Why Stonehenge of England is not one of the seven wonders.
  (D) How the ancient Greeks created the list of ancient wonders.

( ) 2. **Which of the following is TRUE?**
  (A) The Greeks did not know much about Asian culture.
  (B) The Great Wall of China is the last surviving wonder.
  (C) There are two different lists of ancient wonders.
  (D) The seven ancient wonders are frequently visited today.

( ) 3. **It can be inferred from this passage that the writer probably believes that _____.**
  (A) China and England should have their own list of wonders
  (B) the Great Pyramid of Giza is the most beautiful ancient wonder
  (C) the wonders that are on the list were not the only ones around
  (D) the Greeks were the best people in the world to make such a list

There are six international science Olympiads in the world. They are all organized with a simple intention — to _____1_____ global understanding and **mutual**[01] appreciation among young scientists in all countries. Each of the six science Olympiads _____2_____ its specific aims. The aims of the International Mathematical Olympiad (IMO), for example, are three-fold. With **arduous**[02] but interesting math problems, the first aim of the IMO is to discover, to encourage and, most important of all, to challenge _____3_____ gifted young people all over the world. Secondly, it is by **participating**[03] in any IMO contest that young mathematicians of all countries can **foster**[04] friendly _____4_____. Based upon its second aim, more international exchanges are encouraged and established. Any IMO contest brings not only young **mathematicians**[05] together but also their instructors; _____5_____, the IMO has its final aim to create opportunities for the exchange of information on math theories and practices throughout the world.

單字片語補充站

01 mutual [形] 相互的   **04** foster [動] 促進

02 arduous [形] 困難的   **05** mathematician [名] 數學家

03 participate [動] 參與

Quiz

( ) 01. (A) sponsor   (B) promote
      (C) determine   (D) calculate

( ) 02. (A) has   (B) is
      (C) have   (D) are

( ) 03. (A) destructively   (B) effectively
      (C) mutually   (D) mathematically

( ) 04. (A) behaviors   (B) messages
      (C) relations   (D) guests

( ) 05. (A) whereas   (B) nevertheless
      (C) therefore   (D) likewise

Fiction is the name we use for stories that are **make-believe**[01], such as *Harry Potter* or *Alice in the Wonderland*. _____1_____ It can be so close to the truth that it seems as real as something that happened to you this morning. Or, fiction can be as fantastic as the most unbelievable **fairy tale**[02].

Not everything in a fictional story has to be **made up**[03]. _____2_____ You, of course, are real, and the moon is real, and many of the things that you could describe, such as the stars, the wind, and the **pull of gravity**[04], would be real. _____3_____ It would be a trip you took in your imagination.

Nonfiction, on the other hand, is all about true things. _____4_____ Someone's **biography**[05] is nonfiction; so is your autobiography. So are articles in your local newspaper, and school reports on science. _____5_____ Imagine writing history about the 1989 San Francisco earthquake, or a report about a high school sports team. An old proverb says, "Truth is stranger than fiction." Do you think that's true?

單字片語補充站

01 **make-believe** [形] 虛構的　　**04** **pull of gravity** [片] 地心引力

02 **fairy tale** [片] 童話故事　　**05** **biography** [名] 傳記

03 **made up** [片] 虛構的

 **Quiz**

(A) Nothing is made up.

(B) History is nonfiction, too.

(C) But your trip through space would be fiction.

(D) You could write a story in which you fly to the moon.

(E) But fiction isn't always different from the way things usually are.

Unit 02-1: 文章概要及重點理解

　　世界七大奇蹟是在歷史上引起人們驚奇與震驚的七項建築結構的名單。儘管許多古代奇蹟的名單曾被提出，在人們公認的名單裡，七項古代奇蹟包含了吉薩大金字塔、巴比倫空中花園、阿耳忒彌斯神廟、宙斯神像、亞歷山大燈塔、羅得島太陽神銅像和摩索拉斯王陵墓。因為原本是由希臘人所寫成的名單，被選上的古代奇蹟大多都是希臘的、或至少是來自希臘人所熟悉的文明。因此中國長城和英國巨石陣不在名單上也不令人驚訝。無奈因為時間和文明間的交戰，六大古代奇蹟已被摧毀，只有大金字塔存留到今日。每一個古代奇蹟都是古人驚人問題解決能力的紀念碑，他們在現代工程技術還沒發展前，成功地完成了幾個世紀以來一直激發著人們想像力的工程。今日人們依然向這些古代奇蹟尋求靈感，誰知道有多少今日的奇蹟是被這些古代建築物所啟發的呢？

(D) 1. 文章裡沒有提供何種資訊？
　　　A. 七大奇蹟為何依然是靈感的來源
　　　B. 七大奇蹟其中六個不再存在的原因
　　　C. 為何英國巨石陣不在七大奇蹟之中
　　　D. 古希臘人如何創造了古代奇蹟名單

(A) 2. 下列何項敘述為真？
　　　A. 希臘人過去並不清楚亞洲文化
　　　B. 中國長城是唯一留下來的奇蹟
　　　C. 有兩種不同的古代奇蹟名單
　　　D. 人們今日常造訪七大奇蹟

(C) 3. 從文章中可以推斷作者相信：
　　　A. 中國和英國應該有自己的奇蹟名單
　　　B. 吉薩大金字塔是最美的古代奇蹟
　　　C. 在名單上的古代奇蹟並不是唯一的古代奇蹟
　　　D. 製作這樣的奇蹟名單希臘人是世界上最適合的人選

Unit 02-2: 透過克漏字題型強化文法概念

　　世界上有六項國際奧林匹亞科學競賽。他們都是因為一個單純的動機而成立的—為了提倡全世界年輕科學家之間的國際共識和欣賞彼此的能力。六個奧林匹亞科學競賽中每個競賽都有其特定的目標。舉例來說，國際奧林匹亞數學競賽(IMO) 的目標有三個。運用艱鉅卻有趣的數學問題，IMO 的第一個目標是要發掘、鼓勵，還有最重要的，挑戰全世界在數學方面天賦異秉的年輕人。第二，就是藉由參與 IMO 的競賽各個國家的年輕數學家們才能培養友好的關係。基於他的第二個目標，他們鼓勵並且建立了更多的國際交換。任何一個 IMO 競賽不單單只是帶來年輕的數學家讓它們齊聚一堂，更帶來了他們的指導老師；所以，IMO 的終極目標是要創造世界上數學理論實務的資訊交換機會。

1.B　2.A　3.D　4.C　5.C

Unit 02-3: 熟悉篇章的前後銜接關係

　　我們稱那些虛構的故事，像是《哈利波特》和《愛麗絲夢遊仙境》等為小說。**(E) 但小說並不總是和事情原本的樣子不同。**它可以如此貼近現實，就像今天早晨發生在身上的事情一樣真實。小說也可以像最難以相信的童話故事一般夢幻。

　　並非所有在虛構故事中的事物都必須是編造的。**(D) 你可以寫一個你飛到月球的故事。**你，你當然是真的，月亮也是真的，許多你會描寫的東西，像是星星、風和地心引力，都是真的。**(C) 但你的太空旅行會是一篇小說。**它是一個在你想像中的旅行。

　　另一方面，非小說則都是關於真實的事物。**(A) 沒有事物是捏造出來的。**個人的傳記是非小說，你的自傳也是。地方報紙上的新聞、學校的科學報告都是。**(B) 歷史也是非小說。**想像寫1989年舊金山大地震的歷史，或是一個關於高中球隊的報導。就像古老的諺語說的：「真實比小說更奇異」，你同意嗎？

1.E　2.D　3.C　4.A　5.B

History and Culture
歷史文化篇

Unit **03-1:** 文章概要及重點理解
閱讀全文，並回答下列的問題

The first great civilizations of the world developed along the banks of great rivers. From the beginning, conditions in the Nile River Valley in Egypt, and in areas like the Nile River Valley in what is now the Middle East, were favorable for agriculture. It was in river valleys that early people first worked out rules for living together in communities. The earliest rules dealt with irrigation. Cooperation was needed to build systems of dams and canals, leaders were needed to supervise the building, and laws were needed to ensure fair use of materials and water.

The well-watered, fertile soil produced abundant harvests. So fertile was the soil of the Nile Valley that farmers could produce more than enough food for themselves and their families. As a result, surplus goods could be sold. This resulted in the development of trade and commerce, and with these came the exchange of ideas and inventions between people of different regions.

Since there was ample food available, not everyone had to be engaged in farming. Some people left farming to develop arts and crafts. Potters learned to shape clay to make decorative vases; weavers learned to make fabrics and patterns of intricate designs; carpenters learned to build different types of furniture; and architects learned to construct elaborate buildings for government and worship. Thus, civilization and culture grew and prospered in the river valleys of the Middle East.

Quiz

( ) 1. **Which of the following tells us why civilization first developed in the Nile River Valley and in the Middle East?**
(A) It was a major center for trade.
(B) The soil was fertile and produced abundant harvests.
(C) The area had a large population.
(D) People were deeply religious.

( ) 2. **The rise of trade in the ancient world most likely resulted in _____.**
(A) development of a system of numerals to keep business records
(B) widespread use of irrigation systems
(C) the building of large temples to the gods
(D) the domestication of animals

After 1812, white **settlers**[01] began to move west across North America. At first, the settlers and the Indians lived ____1____. However, the number of settlers **increased**[02] greatly every year, and slowly the Indians began to see the white settlers as a danger to their ____2____. To feed themselves, the settlers killed ____3____ wild animals. The Indians, who ____4____ on these animals for food, had to struggle against **starvation**[03]. The settlers also brought with them many **diseases**[04] which were common in white society, but which were new for the Indians. Great numbers of Indians became sick and died. ____5____ 1834 and 1854 the Indian **population**[05] in one area of the country went down from 100,000 to 30,000.

單字片語補充站

01 **settler** [名] 移居者、殖民者

04 **disease** [名] 疾病

02 **increase** [動] 增加

05 **population** [名] 人口

03 **starvation** [名] 飢餓

Quiz

( ) **01.** (A) peaceful   (B) in peace
        (C) peace   (D) happiness

( ) **02.** (A) survival   (B) survive
        (C) survived   (D) survives

( ) **03.** (A) little   (B) less
        (C) more   (D) more and more

( ) **04.** (A) dependent   (B) independent
        (C) depends   (D) depended

( ) **05.** (A) From   (B) Since   (C) To   (D) Between

The Japanese Cherry blossoms, with its **radiate**[01], **delicate**[02], and **transient**[03] beauty, are world **renowned**[04]. ____1____ The blossoming period of Sakura may occur between March to early May according to different weather conditions across the **diverse**[05] **landscape**[06] of Japan's main islands. ____2____ This is the most impressive scenes for most viewers.

Known as Sakura in Japanese, these trees actually have powerful ties to the country's history and culture. Cherry blossoms are considered the **embodiment**[07] of Wabi-Sab philosophy. ____3____ Also, Japanese people **associate**[08] the blooming of the cherry blossom trees with the transience and **nobleness**[09] of human life. ____4____ It is an important occasion for the family, friends, or colleagues to gather together and strengthening bonds. ____5____ It also has been the center of countless events, festivals, and **specialty**[10] tours in Japan.

單字片語補充站

01 radiate [動] 流露、發光　　**06 landscape** [名] 地形景觀

02 delicate [形] 細膩的　　　　**07 embodiment** [名] 體現

03 transient [形] 短暫的　　　　**08 associate** [動] 聯想

04 renowned [形] 著名的　　　　**09 nobleness** [名] 高貴

05 diverse [形] 多樣的　　　　　**10 specialty** [名] 特產、專業

 Quiz

(A) It's a magical moment when small, round shaped flowers fluttering gracefully from the trees.

(B) In spring, people hold 'flower viewing' parties known as 'Hanami' to celebrate the limited flowering period.

(C) In sum, Sakura carries the cultural significance.

(D) They are also the major attraction for tourists.

(E) It is an attitude of accepting the imperfectness of life in ancient Japanese aesthetic ideas.

Unit 03-1: 文章概要及重點理解

　　世界上最早的偉大文明是沿著大河河岸發展的。起初，埃及尼羅河谷及現在在中東具有類似尼羅河谷條件的地區，頗利於農業。早期居住在河谷的人們率先制定出社區共處的定律。最早期的定律正是與灌溉有關。建築水壩、運河等系統需要協力完成。監督建築過程需要領袖，同時也需要法令以確保物資與水源的公平使用。

　　供水良好且肥沃的土壤產量豐盛。正因尼羅河谷土壤肥沃，所以農人們為自已及家人生產的食物超過需求。因此，多餘的物資便能銷售出去。這導致了貿易及商業發展。隨著這些發展也帶來不同區域人們觀念及發明物的交流。

　　由於食物供應充足，因此並非人人都必須務農。有些人便捨棄耕種去發展藝術與工藝。陶土匠學習捏造黏土以製作裝飾用的花瓶；織布者學習紡布以及編織複雜的花紋；木匠學習製作不同款式的傢俱；而建築師學習替政府及宗教祭拜設計精製的建築。因此，在中東河谷的文明與文化逐漸成長茁壯。

(B) 1. 下列何者告訴我們最早的文明是在尼羅河谷及中東地區發展出
　　　　來的？
　　　A. 它是主要貿易中心
　　　B. 那裡土壤肥沃且產量豐盛
　　　C. 那裡的區域人口眾多
　　　D. 人們篤信宗教

(A) 2. 古代貿易的興起很可能導致了？
　　　A. 數字系統的發展以利商業記帳
　　　B. 灌溉系統的廣泛使用
　　　C. 大型廟宇的建立以對眾神朝拜
　　　D. 眷養家畜

Unit 03-2: 透過克漏字題型強化文法概念

一八一二年以後，白種開墾者開始西遷橫越北美洲。起初，這些開墾者與印地安人和平共處。不過，開墾者的人數每年快速增加，印地安人漸漸認為白種人威脅到他們的生存。為了能夠養活自己，這些開墾者開始屠宰愈來愈多的野生動物。依賴這些野生動物為生的印地安人得和饑餓奮鬥。開墾者也帶來了疾病，這些疾病在白人社會裡很普遍，可是對印地安人而言卻是前所未聞的。大量的印地安人生病死亡。一八三四至一八五四年期間美國某地區的印地安人口從十萬人驟降到三萬人。

1.B　2.A　3.D　4.D　5.D

Unit 03-3: 熟悉篇章的前後銜接關係

日本櫻花光輝、細緻、又短暫的美是世界著名的。**(D) 櫻花也是吸引觀光客的亮點。**櫻花的花期可能出現在三月到五月初之間，視日本主要島嶼不同地形的各種天氣狀況而定。**(A) 細小、圓形的櫻花優雅地從樹上落下，是很具有魔力的景緻。**對許多賞花者來說，這是最令人印象深刻的畫面。

櫻花在日文中叫做「Sakura」，而櫻花樹其實和該國的歷史及文化有很深的淵源。櫻花被視為是一種日本哲學「侘寂」的體現。**(E) 它代表一種古老日本美學，是接受生命不完美的態度。**此外，日本人將櫻花和人類生命的短暫與高貴特質聯想在一起。**(B) 在春天，人們會舉辦「賞花會」(Hanami)，藉以慶祝短暫的花期。**它是一個家人、朋友、或同事相聚並且增加聯繫的場合。**(C) 總之，櫻花具有重要的文化意義。**它也是許多在日本活動、節慶、和特殊旅遊行程的重點。

1.D　2.A　3.E　4.B　5.C

Unit 04 **Clothing**
衣著搭配篇

One laundry detergent company certainly now realizes its mistake. It probably wishes that it had asked for the opinion of some Arabic speakers before it started its new advertising program in the Middle East. All of the company's advertisements showed dirty clothes on the left, its box of soap in the middle, and clean clothes on the right. But people read Arabic from right to left, not left to right. For this reason, many potential customers saw the ad and thought, "This soap makes clothes dirty!"

An anthropologist with many years of experience in Brazil, Conrad Philip Kottak noted the advertising for McDonald's when the fast food restaurant first opened in Rio de Janeiro. The advertisements listed several "favorite places where you can enjoy McDonald's products."Clearly, the marketing people were trying to fit their product into Brazilian middle-class culture, but car with the kids." It seems that the writer of this ad never tried to drive up to a fast food restaurant in a neighborhood with no parking places. Also not very helpful was the suggestion to eat McDonald's hamburgers "at a picnic at the beach." This ignored the Brazilian custom of consuming cold things, such as beer, soft drinks, ice cream, and ham and cheese sandwiches, at a beach picnic. It's hard enough to keep sand off an ice cream cone; not to mention Brazilians do not consider a hot, greasy hamburger proper beach food.

( ) 1. **The laundry detergent company made a mistake because it thought that _____.**
   (A) people read Arabic from right to left
   (B) people read Arabic from left to right
   (C) clothes in Middle East got dirty more easily than in other place
   (D) the Arabic were not so cleanly as the Americans

( ) 2. **It can be inferred from the first paragraph that _____.**
   (A) the company made smart investigation about the Arabic culture
   (B) the company didn't ask for the opinion of Arabic speakers
   (C) a new product will definitely gain popularity in a foreign country
   (D) no advertisement will be successful in a foreign country unless its writer can speak the language

____1____food and **shelter**[01], man has another important need. It is clothing. Man wears clothing for at least three purposes, ____2____, for **protection**[02], for **decoration**[03], and for **modesty**[04]. In other words, clothing can protect us from the rain and from the sun. It can also make us look handsome or beautiful. Moreover, it can ____3____ the manners we have, and it shows our personal preferences toward clothing, for fashion tastes ____4____.

A person who is active and young may like to wear clothing which is colorful and brighter, while a person who is more introverted or at an older age may like to dress in a plain and darker style. On the other hand, an official who is in charge of a company is more likely to tidy himself up. ____5____, he looks professional and **dynamic**[05]. ____6____, a person who does not dress up or at least get a tidy look may strike other people as a lazy man. To conclude, man may wear clothing for different purposes. But, the clothing a man wears can reveal his personality. Therefore, how to wear and what to wear is important because what you wear shows your ____7____ and how you wear reveals your characteristic.

單字片語補充站

01 shelter [名] 居所、庇護所

02 protection [名] 保護

03 decoration [名] 裝飾

04 modesty [名] 端莊、謙虛

05 dynamic [形] 有活力的

Quiz

( ) 01. (A) According to (B) In addition to
(C) Compare to (D) Beside

( ) 02. (A) namely (B) this is to say
(C) no doubt (D) in other words

( ) 03. (A) redefine (B) refine (C) reflash (D) reflect

( ) 04. (A) varies (B) vary (C) differs (D) changes

( ) 05. (A) In doing so (B) By the way
(C) By doing so (D) On doing so

( ) 06. (A) On the other words (B) At the meanwhile
(C) That is to say (D) On the contrary

( ) 07. (A) liking (B) flavor (C) casual (D) favorite

Ever since the beginning of history, human beings have learned to **cover**[01] their bodies with clothes. ____1____, every year fashion designers create billions of clothes, shoes, and **accessories**[02] for a **discerning**[03] and **fickle**[04] body of consumers. Although clothes are made in **various**[05] styles, ____2____: They keep us warm in winter and protect us from the **heat**[06] in summer.

____3____ . In the first place, they are inexpensive, **durable**[07] and comfortable. Secondly, when dirty, they're easy to take care of. ____4____ . Wearing a T-shirt and jeans makes you feel youthful and full of **vigor**[08]. Although I sometimes wear a shirt for a change, ____5____.

單字片語補充站

01 cover [動] 遮蓋

02 accessories [名] 配件、飾品

03 discerning
[形] 有識別力、有品味的

04 fickle [形] 善變的

05 various [形] 不同的

06 heat [名] 熱氣、熱度

07 durable [形] 耐久持用的

08 vigor [名] 活力、精力

Quiz

(A) their functions are almost the same

(B) I still feel more comfortable in a T-shirt and jeans

(C) As a student, I prefer T-shirts and jeans

(D) Strongly influenced by the concept that "fine feathers make fine birds"

(E) I don't need to iron them before wearing them

Unit 04-1: 文章概要及重點理解

　　某家洗衣粉公司現在一定了解它所犯的錯誤了。它可能會希望在中東推出它的洗衣粉廣告之前，事先徵詢過一些說阿拉伯語的人的意見。這家公司呈現其洗衣粉的廣告一向都是依照下列的次序：髒衣服在左邊，一盒肥皂在中間，乾淨的衣服在右邊。但是，阿拉伯話的讀法是由右至左，不是由左至右。因此本來有意買此種洗衣粉的阿拉伯顧客，看了此廣告後，都認為「這種肥皂使衣服變髒了！」

　　人類學家康瑞克德先生住在巴西多年了，他注意到速食店在里約熱內盧推出的第一支廣告。此廣告的內容建議了幾個可以好好享受麥當勞產品的地方。設計此廣告的行銷人員，很明顯是以巴西中產階級人士為其產品推銷對象。但是，他們犯了一些錯誤。這個廣告的一個建議是「當你開車載小孩出去玩的時候，請到麥當勞來用餐。」寫這個廣告的作者，似乎從沒嘗試過開車到里約熱內盧附近的速食店用餐，因為他不知道在那裡停車是很困難的。另一個廣告也不是很成功，此廣告建議巴西人在海邊野餐的時候，吃麥當勞的漢堡。此廣告忽略了巴西人在海邊野餐的習慣是吃冷的食物，例如：啤酒、料、冰淇淋、火腿乳酪夾三明治。巴西人要避免不讓冰淇淋甜筒沾到海邊的沙已經很不容易了，更不用說他們認為熱熱的、油膩的漢堡，不是理想的海邊食物。

(B) 1. 這家洗衣粉公司的錯誤是因為它認為：
　　　A. 人們讀阿拉伯文是由右至左
　　　B. 人們讀阿拉伯文是由左至右
　　　C. 衣服在中東比在其他地方更容易弄髒
　　　D. 阿拉伯人不像美國人那麼愛乾淨

(B) 2. 從第一段文章可以推斷出：
　　　A. 這家公司對阿拉伯文化做了正確的調查
　　　B. 這家公司沒有徵詢說阿拉伯語的人的意見
　　　C. 一種新產品一定會在國外受歡迎
　　　D. 除非寫廣告的人會說某一國的語言，否則此廣告不能在該國成功的

Unit **04-2:** 透過克漏字題型強化文法概念

　　在食物和居所之外，人有另一個重要的需求——服裝。人們穿衣服至少是為了這三個目的——保護、裝飾、表示莊重。換句話說，衣服可以保護我們不被日曬雨淋。也可以使我們看來英俊或美麗。此外，服裝更可以反映我們的風度，並展示出我們對於服裝的個人喜好，因為時尚品味是因人而異的。

　　積極和年輕的人可能會穿多彩和較亮麗的衣服，而較內向或是較年長的人則傾向穿樸素和較暗沉的服裝。另一方面，掌管公司的職員或領導人喜歡將自己打扮整齊。藉由如此，他看起來更專業有活力。他可以輕易地為他組織的成員樹立榜樣。相反地，不打扮和沒有整潔外表的人會讓別人覺得是懶惰的人。總括來說，人會為了不同的目的而穿衣。但人穿的衣服會顯露出他的性格。因此，如何穿和穿什麼便很重要，因為你的穿著顯露你的喜好、你怎麼穿會顯露你的個性。

1.B　2.A　3.D　4.B　5.C　6.D　7.A

Unit **04-3:** 熟悉篇章的前後銜接關係

　　自有歷史開始以來，人類已經學會用衣服遮蓋他們的身體。**(D)強烈受到「人要衣裝、佛要金裝」觀念的影響**，每一年服裝設計師製造出數十億的衣服、鞋子和配件給挑剔和善變的消費者。雖然衣服做成不同的款式，**(A)它們的功能大都是相同**。它們在冬天使我們保持溫暖，在夏天保護我們避免暑熱。

　　(C)做為一個學生，我比較喜歡運動衫和牛仔褲。首先，它們不貴、耐穿又舒適；其次，髒的時候也很容易處理，**(E)我不用在穿之前先把它們燙好**。穿上運動衫和一條牛仔褲使你充滿了青春的活力。雖然我有時也穿一件襯衫換換口味，**(B)但我仍然覺得穿牛仔褲和運動衫比較舒服**。

1.D　2.A　3.C　4.E　5.B

Unit 05 Economic Conditions
商業經濟篇

 Unit 05-1：文章概要及重點理解
閱讀全文，並回答下列的問題

Specialists in marketing have studied how to make people buy more food in a supermarket. They do all kinds of things that you do not even notice. For example, the simple, ordinary food that everybody must buy, like bread, milk, flour, and vegetable oil, is spread all over the store. You have to walk by all the more interesting-and more expensive-things in order to find what you need. The more expensive food is in packages with brightly-colored pictures. This food is placed at eye level so you see it and want to buy it. The things that you have to buy anyway are usually located on a higher or lower shelf. However, candy and other things that children like are on lower shelves. One study showed that when a supermarket moved four products from floor to eye level, it sold 78 percent more.

Quiz

( ) 1. In a supermarket the simple and ordinary food is
_____.

(A) placed at eye level
(B) placed on a higher shelf
(C) located on a lower shelf
(D) spread all over the store

( ) 2. Packages that have brightly-colored pictures are
_____.

(A) the more expensive food
(B) cheap food
(C) ordinary food
(D) children's food

( ) 3. A supermarket can increase sales by _____.

(A) selling more expensive products
(B) moving products from floor to eye level
(C) packing goods brightly
(D) cheating customers

( ) 4. Specialists in marketing know a lot about _____.

(A) consumer psychology
(B) consumers' eyesight
(C) consumers' purchasing power
(D) the art of packaging

Unit 05-2: 透過克漏字題型強化文法概念
閱讀全文，並選出空格中該填入的字彙

To **manage**[01] your money, look into the future. What is it ____1____ you want? Once you decide, you can set goals ____2____ . Then you'll ____3____ to **squander**[02] your money.

You should have short-term, **intermediate**[03]-term and long-term goals. Short-term goals are things you want in less than a year, like buying new clothes or taking a vacation. Intermediate-term goals can ____4____ in one to five years. Long-term goals look ahead 5 to 10 years ____5____ . These are things like going to college or buying an apartment.

Do you ever wonder where all the money in your wallet goes? If you do, maybe it's time to examine your spending habits. Think about **purchases**[04] before you make them. Ask yourself questions like these:

- Can I do without it?
- Can I continue to use what I already have?
- Can I **substitute**[05] something less expensive?
- Is it a want or a need?
- Why do I want to buy it?

Learn to say "no" to **unnecessary**[06] purchases. Then you'll have money to buy the things you really want or need.

單字片語補充站

01 manage [動] 管理

02 squander [動] 揮霍、浪費

03 intermediate [形] 中間的

04 purchase [動] 購買

05 substitute [動] 取代

06 unnecessary [形] 不必要的

Quiz

( ) **01.** (A) when　(B) which　(C) for　(D) since

( ) **02.** (A) to get　　　　(B) to get it
　　　　(C) and getting　　(D) getting it

( ) **03.** (A) likely　　　　(B) be less likely
　　　　(C) like　　　　　(D) less like

( ) **04.** (A) accommodate　　(B) be accomplished
　　　　(C) accomplish　　　(D) be accommodated

( ) **05.** (A) by the way　(B) at all　(C) instead　(D) or longer

Banks are not ordinarily prepared to pay out all **accounts**[01]; ____1____. If **depositors**[02] should come to fear that a bank is not sound, that it cannot pay off all its depositors, ____2____. If they did, the bank could not pay all accounts. ____3____. Mrs. Elsie Vaught has told us of a terrifying **bank run**[03] that she experienced. One day in December of 1925, several banks failed to open in a city where Mrs. Vaught lived. The other banks **anticipated**[04] a run the next day, and so the officers of the bank in which Mrs. Vaught worked had enough funds on hand to pay off as many depositors as might apply. The officers simply **instructed**[05] the **tellers**[06] to pay on demand. ____4____. The length of the line **convinced**[07] many that the bank could not possibly pay off everyone. People began to push and then to fight for places near the tellers windows. Clothing was torn and **limbs**[08] broken, but the **jam**[09] continued for hours. The power of the **panic**[10] atmosphere is evident in the fact that two tellers, ____5____. Mrs. Vaught says that she had difficulty restraining herself from doing the same.

單字片語補充站

01 account [名] 帳戶

02 depositor [名] 存戶

03 bank run [動] 擠兌

04 anticipate [動] 期望、預期

05 instruct [動] 命令、吩咐

06 teller [名] 櫃員

07 convince [動] 說服

08 limbs [名] 四肢

09 jam [名] 此指擁擠的人潮

10 panic [名] 驚慌

 **Quiz**

(A) then that fear might cause all its depositors to appear on the same day

(B) though they knew that the bank was sound and could pay out all depositors, nevertheless withdrew the funds in their own accounts

(C) they rely on depositors not to demand payment all at the same time

(D) However, if they did not all appear at once, then there would always be funds to pay those who wanted their money when they wanted it

(E) Next morning, a crowd gathered in the bank and on the sidewalk

Answer 中文翻譯及參考解答

Unit 05-1: 文章概要及重點理解

　　行銷專家研究過，如何才能使人們在超級市場中買更多的食物。他們做了各種一般人察覺不到的事。例如，每個人都要買的簡單普通的食物，像是麵包、牛奶、麵粉和蔬菜油被散布在商店的各個角落。要買到你需要的東西，就必須走過比較有趣，而且也比較貴的東西。比較貴的食物，會用有鮮艷圖案的包裝。這種食物會放在你眼睛可平視的高度，進而讓你看到，並且引起購物慾。那些你一定會買的東西，通常就放在較高，或較低的架子上。然而，小孩喜歡的糖果和其他東西，則都擺在較低的架子上。有一項研究顯示，當超市將四項產品，由地板移至眼睛能平視的高度時，其銷售量便增加了百分之七十八。

(D) 1. 在超級市場中，簡單且普通的食物 _____ 。
　　　　A. 被放在眼睛能平視的高度　　B. 被放在較高的架子上
　　　　C. 位於較低的架子上　　　　　**D. 散布在商店的各個角落**

(A) 2. 使用有鮮艷圖案的包裝的是_____。
　　　　A. 較貴的食物　　　　　　　B. 便宜的食物
　　　　C. 普通的食物　　　　　　　　D. 小孩的食物

(B) 3. 超級市場可藉由_____增加其銷售量。
　　　　A. 賣更多昂貴的產品
　　　　B. 將商品由地板移至眼睛可平視的高度
　　　　C. 將商品包裝得很鮮艷
　　　　D. 欺騙顧客

(A) 4. 行銷專家很清楚_____。
　　　　A. 消費者的心理　　　　　　B. 消費者的視力
　　　　C. 消費者的購買力　　　　　　D. 包裝的藝術

Unit 05-2: 透過克漏字題型強化文法概念

　　若要管理錢財，眼光要放遠。你要的是什麼？一旦作了決定後，你可以設定目標去達成，這樣比較不會浪費錢。

　　你應該要有短期、中期和長期的目標。短期目標是你在一年內想要的東西，像是買新衣服或是去度假。中期目標可以在一到五年內完成。長期目標則前瞻五到十年或更久的時間，像進大學或是買一層公寓之類的事情。

你曾懷疑錢包裡的錢都到哪裡去了嗎？如果有，也許是檢視花錢習慣的時候了。在出手購買前要三思，問自己這些問題：

- 沒有它行嗎？
- 可以繼續使用我原本有的東西嗎？
- 可以用比較便宜的東西取代嗎？
- 這是想要的東西還是需要的東西？
- 我為什麼想買它？

學習對非必要的東西說「不」，你就會有錢去購買真正想要或需要的東西了。

1.B　2.B　3.B　4.B　5.D

Unit **05-3: 熟悉篇章的前後銜接關係**

各家銀行平常並不準備支付所有的帳戶，**(C)它們指望存款人絕不會同時要求支付**。萬一存款人恐懼某家銀行不健全，而且不能支付所有的存款人，**(A)那麼那種恐懼可能造成所有存款人同一天出現**。如果他們這樣做，銀行就無法支付那些需要提款的人。**(D)然而，如果他們不同時出現，當人們需要他們的錢時將永遠會有基金去支付它們**。愛爾喜·佛特夫人告訴我們她親身經歷的一家銀行令人驚嚇的擠兌。在一九二五某一天，她居住的城市有數家銀行沒有營業。其他銀行預期隔天會有擠兌，所以佛特夫人任職的銀行的長官準備足夠資金去支付所有可能申請提款的人。銀行官員只訓示出納員依請求付款。**(E)第二天早上，一大群人聚集在銀行內和外面的人行道**。排隊人數的長度使許多人相信這家銀行不能支付每個人。人們開始推擠以便站到接近出納員窗口的地方。衣服被扯破、手腳也受傷了，但是這次的推擠持續達數小時之久。驚慌氣氛的強度由以下事實可知，有二位出納員**(B)雖然明知該銀行健全並能支付所有的存款人，但他們也提領他們在戶頭的存款**。佛特夫人說她實在很難阻止自己不去提款。

1.C　2.A　3.D　4.E　5.B

Unit 06 **Matters of Life**
生老病死篇

Unit **06-1**: 文章概要及重點理解
閱讀全文，並回答下列的問題

Many developed nations are facing the issues of the aging population. To deal with potential problems of an aging society, the government of Taiwan has launched a long-term care plan. The Ministry of Health and Welfare (MOHW) has been promoting the National Ten-year Long-term Care Plan 2.0 since 2005. More people can have access to resources of the public long-term care system.

One feature of the long-term care management project is that it offers comprehensive community-based care service. The government coordinated the local long-term care facilities so that they can provide the services that caters to the long-term care service applicants' need.

Besides, MOHW made dementia care services available to people suffering from the health issue and their families. By November 2018, 73 Integrated Dementia Care Centers were established. They offer diversified rehabilitation services to the civilians. The welfare of home-caregiving staff is another focus of Long-term Care Plan 2.0. The homecare workers got a salary raise, which led to an encouraging job retention rate in 2018. The MOHW also works with Ministry of Labor to expand respite care services for families with foreign caregivers. If the foreign caregiver is temporarily unable to provide care service, the family of a disabled individual can apply for the service. The long-term care service is still evolving. Hopefully, better management of the local long-term care institutions can make the system more efficient.

Quiz

( ) 1. **How many features of 'Long-term Care Plan 2.0' have been mentioned in the passage?**
   (A) Two.   (B) Three.
   (C) Four.   (D) Five.

( ) 2. **According to the passage, what happened in 2018?**
   (A) The Ministry of Health and Welfare launched Long-term Care 2.0 plan.
   (B) The first dementia care center in Taiwan was established.
   (C) The first foreign home-caregiver was introduced to Taiwan.
   (D) The MOHW improved the welfare of homecare workers.

( ) 3. **What can be inferred from the last part of the passage?**
   (A) Long-term Care Plan 2.0 faced opposition.
   (B) The MOHW failed to collaborate with Ministry of Labor.
   (C) The government will keep improving the long-term care system.
   (D) The working environment for foreign caregivers might become harsh.

One of the **poignant**[01] trends of U.S. life is the gradual **devaluation**[02] of older people. The young largely ignore the old or treat them with a kind of **totalitarian**[03] cruelty. It is as though the aged ____1____ race to which the young never belong. It is not just **cruelty**[04] and ____2____ cause such **ageism**[05]. It is also the nature of modern western culture. In some societies, the past of the adults is the future of each new generation, and therefore is taught and respected. Thus, **primitive**[06] families stay together and **cherish**[07] their ____3____ . But in modern U.S., the generations live apart, and social changes are so rapid that to learn about the past is considered **unsuitable**[08]. In this situation, new in history, the aged ____4____ generation, the carriers of a ____5____ culture. **Ironically**[09], millions of these shunted-aside old people are remarkably able: medicine has kept them young at the same time that technology has made them ____6____ date.

單字片語補充站

01 poignant
[形] 令人強烈哀傷的、令人辛酸的

02 devaluation [名] 貶值

03 totalitarian [形] 極權主義的

04 cruelty [名] 殘忍

05 ageism [名] 年齡歧視

06 primitive [形] 原始的

07 cherish [動] 珍惜、尊重

08 unsuitable
[形] 不適合的、不合時宜的

09 ironically [副] 諷刺地

 Quiz

( ) **01.** (A) are an alien　　　　(B) were alienated
　　　　(C) were an alien　　　　(D) were an alienating

( ) **02.** (A) difference that　　　(B) indifference
　　　　(C) indifference that　　(D) difference

( ) **03.** (A) olders (B) elderly　　(C) elders　　　(D) old

( ) **04.** (A) are a strangely isolated (B) is a strangely isolated
　　　　(C) are a strange-isolated　(D) is an isolating strange

( ) **05.** (A) dyeing (B) dying　　(C) dead　　　(D) deadly

( ) **06.** (A) in　　　(B) to　　　(C) out of　　(D) up to

In recent years, there have been cases of old people dying alone in their apartments, not being found for several weeks. ____1____ . More **frightening**[01] are the **numerous**[02] horror stories about the ill treatment of the senior citizens who live in nursing homes of poor quality.

____2____ . Nowadays, however, society is much more **complex**[03] and people find it hard to **cope with**[04] the pressures of modern life. ____3____ . This problem is also growing along with the **overall**[05] aging of the population. In my opinion, the government can solve the problem by **investing**[06] more money in building up better-**quality**[07] **nursing homes**[08]. ____4____ , which should not **fade away**[09] with the times. ____5____ .

單字片語補充站

01 frightening [形] 嚇人的
02 numerous [形] 大量的、數量多的
03 complex [形] 複雜的
04 cope with [片] 處理、應付
05 overall [形] 全面的、全部的

06 invest [動] 投資
07 quality [名] 品質
08 nursing home [片] 安養院
09 fade away [片] 消失

 Quiz

(A) Besides, we should promote the traditional virtue of filial piety

(B) The result is that many families are unable to properly care for their senior members

(C) Senior citizens have contributed their best years to their country, society and families, and they deserve dignity and proper care during the last stage of life

(D) In the past, it was traditionally the responsibility of adult children to take care of their aging family members

(E) Besides, we notice that the elderly form a large proportion of homeless people on city streets

Unit 06-1: 文章概要及重點理解

　　許多已開發國家都面臨到人口老化的問題。為了處理高齡化社會的潛在問題，臺灣的政府已經發起了長期照護計畫。衛生福利部從2005年開始就在推動國家十年長期照護2.0計畫。更多人可以用到公共長期照護系統的資源。

　　　這個長期照護管理計畫的其中一項特徵就是，它提供全面的、以社區為基礎的照護服務。政府協調規劃各個長期照護設施，以便提供更多符合長照服務申請者需求的服務項目。

　　此外，衛生福利部提供失智症照護服務給患者和他們的家人。截至2018年11月為止，已經有73間整合失智症照護中心成立。他們提供國民各種復健的服務。長照2.0計畫的另外一個焦點是居家照顧服務者的福利。這些居家照顧工作者獲得加薪，在2018年有更高的留任率，令人欣慰。衛生福利部也和勞動部合作來擴大提供喘息服務給有外籍看護的家庭。如果外籍看護暫時無法提供照護服務，需照顧身心障礙者的家庭可以申請這項服務。長期照護服務仍在逐漸演進。希望更好的機構管理方式可以讓長期照護服務系統更加有效率。

(B) 1. 在文章中提到了幾項「長照2.0」的特色？
　　　A. 兩項。　　　　　　　　**B. 三項。**
　　　C. 四項。　　　　　　　　D. 五項。

(D) 2. 根據本文，2018年發生了什麼事？
　　　A. 衛生福利部啟動了長照2.0計畫。
　　　B. 台灣第一間失智症患者照護中心成立。
　　　C. 第一位外籍居家看護被引進台灣。
　　　D. 衛生福利部改善了居家照護者福利。

(C) 3. 由本文最後一部分可推測出下列何者？
　　　A. 長照2.0遭到反對。
　　　B. 衛生福利部無法和勞動部合作。
　　　C. 政府會持續改進長期照護的系統。
　　　D. 外籍居家看護的工作環境將會變得更加嚴峻。

Unit 06-2: 透過克漏字題型強化文法概念

　　美國生活一個令人感傷的趨勢，就是老年人越來越不受重視。年輕人若不是根本忽略老年人的存在，要不然就是以一種近似極權主義的殘忍來對待他們。老年人就好像是異族一樣，年輕人絕對和他們井水不犯河水。造成這種年齡歧視的原因，不僅是殘忍，還有漠不關心的因素在內。這也是現代西方文化的本質。在某些社會當中，成年人所經歷的過往，就是新生代的未來，因此會教小孩學習這個過程，也會尊重這段過往。因此，早期的家庭都是同聚一堂，而且很尊重長者。但是今天在美國，不同代的人不住在一起，而且社會改變快速，以至於人們認為根本不必學習歷史。在這種情況下，（這種情況是歷史上前所未見的），老年人變成莫名其妙被孤立的一群人，也是一個垂死文化的媒介。諷刺的是，數以百萬這種被擱置一旁的老人其實非常健全：藥物保持他們的青春，但同時科技卻使他們過時。

1.C　2.C　3.C　4.A　5.B　6.C

Unit 06-3: 熟悉篇章的前後銜接關係

　　近幾年來，有好幾件老人獨自死於自家處所，卻在好幾個星期才被發現的案例。**(E)除此之外，我們也注意到在流浪的街友當中，有很大的比例是老人。**更嚇人的是，住在低水準安養院的老人，受到虐待的恐怖案件層出不窮。

　　(D)就過去的傳統而言，照顧年老的家人是孩子們長大成人後的責任。然而，當今的社會比從前要複雜的多，很多人覺得要處理現代生活帶來的壓力非常不容易。**(B)結果，很多家庭都不能好好地照顧家中的長輩。**這個問題也隨著整體人口的老化而日益嚴重。以我之見，政府可以透過投資更多經費、興建更好的安養院來解決這個問題。**(A)再者，我們要推行固有的孝順美德，好讓這美德不隨時間而流失。(C)老人家對國家、社會、家庭都貢獻了他們的黃金歲月，應該在人生的最後階段享有尊嚴和妥善的照顧。**

1.E　2.D　3.B　4.A　5.C

Unit 07 Juvenile Delinquency
少年犯罪篇

Unit 07-1: 文章概要及重點理解
閱讀全文，並回答下列的問題

For some unknown reason, there are far more teenagers in the cities of Taichung and Kaohsiung who are fond of midnight drag racing than there are in other cities. The juvenile motorcyclists, who dash along city streets in groups at life-threatening speeds and with deafening noise, are a nightmare for many citizens. Crackdowns are conducted by the city authorities whenever the racing becomes rampant. And the result? The streets become quiet for some time after each crackdown. The "racers", however, reappear as soon as they think the police are less attentive.

It is not very difficult to figure out why the youths never seem to lose their infatuation with such a dangerous act. Most of them are conceited and self-centered, seeking after thrill or excitement. They have little respect for law and order and want to be treated like heroes. What makes the situation more tragic is today's educators' "democratic" attitude. They keep advising parents and teachers to be nice to the young. "Children need love and care", the educators say. So what do the police usually do with those arrested drag racers? Often, the punishment is nothing but a lecture. Also, the parents and the teachers can do nothing about them, fearing that they might be endangered by the racers' rebellious temperament.

While we agree that children need care and love, we also do believe too many kids are spoiled, which makes them arrogant and uncontrollable, and may make it easier for them to go astray. In fact, to love a child also includes what's necessary to make him or her a well-behaved person. The saying "Spare the rod and spoil the child" sounds completely out-dated in a society where "love" is said to be all-important in education.

 **Quiz**

( ) 1. **According to this article, the drag racers _____.**
  (A) observe traffic regulations
  (B) like to wear helmets
  (C) never seem to lose love in drag racing
  (D) put a high premium on law and order

( ) 2. **According to the article, the author implies _____.**
  (A) teachers should receive punishment for not disciplining their students for misbehavior
  (B) parents should give their children physical punishment whenever they behave badly
  (C) city authorities should shut their eyes to the dangerous behavior of those reckless drag racers
  (D) it's proper discipline as well as love and care that contributes to a well-behaved child

The government has recently ____1____ its latest Crime **Survey**[01]. The survey **involved**[02] people aged between 16 and 59. ____2____ the report, in England and Wales, there has been a ____3____ in use of powder **cocaine**[03] and **ecstasy**[04]. The drug misuse **statistics**[05] shows a highest ____4____ total of Class A drug use since 1996.

According to the **officials**[06], the ____5____ has been caused by a "genuine rise in Class A drug use" among teenagers and people ____6____ their early twenties. Around 8.7% of young adults took a class A drug in the last year. About 10.4% of 20 to 24-year-olds used such drugs, too.

____7____, the official **figures**[07] showed a **record-high**[08] number of drug deaths in England and Wales. Most of the **victims**[09] died for ____8____ opiates such as heroin. Also, cocaine deaths have **doubled**[10] over the last three years. ____9____ the government's focus on reducing class A drug use, the significant increase in such cases among young people since 2012 has still raised ____10____.

單字片語補充站

01 **survey** [名] 調查

02 **involve** [動] 涉及

03 **cocaine** [名] 古柯鹼

04 **ecstasy** [名] 搖頭丸

05 **statistics** [名] 數據

06 **official** [名] 官員

07 **figure** [名] 數據

08 **record-high** [形] 破紀錄的

09 **victim** [名] 受害者

10 **double** [動] 加倍

Quiz

( ) 01. (A) relied (B) relieved (C) released (D) reformed

( ) 02. (A) Due to (B) Owing to (C) According to (D) Contrary to

( ) 03. (A) rise   (B) raise   (C) rose   (D) arise

( ) 04. (A) record   (B) recorded   (C) recording(D) records

( ) 05. (A) deduction (B) induction (C) decrease (D) increase

( ) 06. (A) in   (B) on   (C) at   (D) by

( ) 07. (A) Contrarily (B) In sum (C) Fortunately (D) What's worse

( ) 08. (A) mistaking (B) misusing (C) misplacing (D) misleading

( ) 09. (A) Despite (B) In spite (C) Although   (D) Nevertheless

( ) 10. (A) hands (B) funds (C) concerns   (D) awareness

People often picture a juvenile **cybercriminal**[01] as a super-tech **savvy**[02]. ____1____

However, a recent research has a different conclusion. Many hacker kids may not be that **isolated**[03] in the real world. They actually tend to show qualities as other children who engage in troubled behaviors out in the **offline**[04] world.

____2____ However, hacking can just involve **rudimentary**[05] computer skills. The entry point may be just guessing someone's password to get into their email account. That is, hacking may not be that different from traditional **delinquent**[06] behaviors like shoplifting or other types of petty **theft**[07].

____3____ The outcome shows that teens who become hackers have several common characteristics. Boys are more likely to turn to cybercrimes than their female **counterpart**[08]. ____4____

Experts pointed out that schools need to take measures to **mitigate**[09] the risks from teen hackers. Cyber-awareness campaign should be promoted on campus. ____5____ There should be more 'juvenile crime **rehabilitation**[10] counselors' to convince cyber-hackers to put their talent to more productive use.

單字片語補充站

01 **cybercriminal**
[名] 網路犯罪

02 **savvy** [名] 理解、專精

03 **isolated** [形] 孤立的

04 **offline** [形] 網路之外的

05 **rudimentary** [形] 基本的

06 **delinquent**
[形] 違法的、不良的

07 **theft** [名] 偷竊

08 **counterpart** [名] 相對應的人

09 **mitigate** [動] 減輕、緩和

10 **rehabilitation** [名] 復原

Quiz

(A) Thomas Holt, a cybercrime expert at Michigan State University, pointed out that the society has a stereotype that a hacker is a lone kid of sophisticated computer-user.

(B) Besides, educators should figure out the aptitude of these students and help to put them on the right track.

(C) Also, teens are also more likely to become hackers if their friends like to frighten or intimidate people 'just for fun.'

(D) The new study led by Dr. Holt examined cyber-security crimes within a broader pool of world-wide data on juvenile delinquency.

(E) The nerdy-looked teenager may be typing in chamber with dim light alone.

Unit 07-1: 文章概要及重點理解

不知為什麼，台中及高雄市區喜歡在半夜飆車的青少年比其他城市多很多。這些年輕的機車騎士，成群結隊在街道上拼命狂奔，發出震耳欲聾的噪音，是許多市民的夢魘。每當飆車猖獗時，市政府當局就會進行取締。那結果呢？每次掃蕩後，街道就會安靜一段時間。但是，當這些「飆車族」認為警方較不注意時，他們就會馬上又重現街道。

不難理解青少年為什麼會對這麼危險的舉動深深著迷，熱度似乎不曾減退。他們大部分都很自負，而且以自我為中心，喜歡尋求快感和刺激。他們不太尊重法律及秩序，希望被視為英雄。而現今教育者「民主的」態度讓情況更可悲。他們一直建議父母和老師要對小孩好。教育者說小孩需要愛及關懷。所以警方通常如何處置那些被逮捕的飆車族呢？多半的情況只是訓個話作為處罰。此外，父母和老師對他們無可奈何，害怕他們因飆車族的反叛性格而受到傷害。

儘管我們同意小孩需要關懷和愛，我們也確實相信有很多小孩被寵壞了，他們變得桀驁不馴，而且可能會讓他們很容易就誤入歧途。事實上，愛小孩就表示，要採取必要的行動，讓他們成為行為端正的人。在這個所謂以「愛」為教育重點的社會裡，「不打不成器」這句俗語，聽來已經完全過時了。

(C) 1. 根據這篇文章，飆車族：
　　　A. 遵守交通規則　　　　　　B. 喜歡戴安全帽
　　　C. **似乎不會失去對競速的熱愛**　D. 十分重視法律和秩序

(D) 2. 根據這篇文章，作者暗示：
　　　A. 沒有管教好學生的老師應受到處罰
　　　B. 小孩一犯錯父母就應給予體罰
　　　C. 市府當局應該對肆無忌憚的飆車族視而不見
　　　D. **適當的紀律和愛與照顧都同樣是養成品行端正小孩的因素**

Unit 07-2: 透過克漏字題型強化文法概念

政府最近發佈了最新的犯罪調查。此項調查涵蓋了16歲到59歲的民眾。根據此項報告，在英格蘭和威爾斯，古柯鹼和搖頭丸的使用有增加的趨勢。藥物濫用的數據顯示，A級毒品的使用率創下1996年以來的新高。

官員表示，藥物濫用的增加，主要是因為青少年和二十出頭的年輕人對「A級毒品濫用」的程度增加。去年大約有8.7%的20歲以下年輕人使用A級毒品。在20至24歲的年輕人中，大約有10.4%的人濫用了這類藥品。

更糟的是，官方數據顯示出，在英格蘭和威爾斯藥物濫用致命的人數來到新高。大部分的受害者死於海洛因這類的鴉片劑。此外，古柯鹼致命案例在過去三年倍增。儘管政府致力於減少A級毒品的使用，從2012年以來年輕人藥物濫用的案件增加，還是令人擔憂。

1.C　2.C　3.A　4.B　5.D　6.A　7.D　8.B　9.A　10.C

Unit **07-3: 熟悉篇章的前後銜接關係**

人們常常會想像青少年網路犯罪者是科技專家。**(E) 這個看起來像個書呆子的青少年可能是獨自在燈光昏暗的房間裡面打字。**

但是，最近的研究有不同的結論。很多青少年駭客並不是在真實世界裡面那樣孤立的。他們其實會表現出和其他在真實世界裡面行為偏差的青少年相似的特徵。

(A) 密西根州大學的網路犯罪專家，湯姆士·赫特指出，社會有個刻板印象，認為駭客是有極佳電腦能力的孤僻少年。但是，只要有基礎的電腦應用能力就可能從事駭客行為了。剛開始可能只是猜測某人的密碼，竊取電子信箱帳號資訊而已。也就是說，駭客行為其實和順手牽羊這種小罪之間，沒有太大的差異。

(D) 赫特博士主持的新研究，檢視全球青少年犯罪的統計資量。結果顯示，成為駭客的青少年有些共通的特質。男孩比女孩更具有成為駭客的傾象。**(C) 此外，如果青少年身邊的朋友喜歡「為了好玩」而去嚇唬別人，他們成為駭客的可能也會更高。**

專家指出，學校應該要採取措施減少青少年駭客帶來的風險。校園裡應推廣網路安全意識相關的運動。**(B) 此外，教師應該了解這些學生的潛能，並且幫他們走回正途。**應該要有更多幫助「青少年犯罪反省諮詢師」來說服網路駭客將他們的能力用於更有有意義的面向。

1.E　2.A　3.D　4.C　5.B

Unit 08 Gender Issues
兩性關係篇

Unit 01-1: 文章概要及重點理解
閱讀全文，並回答下列的問題

While dating apps are everywhere, the relationship apps are gaining popularity. These apps aim to teach people to 'love better' has gradually become an alternative for couples that are seeking for marital counseling. Take the app "Lasting" for example. This app is based on suggestions from leading relationship psychologists specializing in couple therapy and more than 300 marriage studies. By paying $11.99 per month, users can get reminders to do little things like texting the partner an expression of gratitude at a certain time of day. The app can also guide users through big things like how to start a conversation about infidelity. "The app is like a third, neutral party that both parties can rely on, and the we can realize where our needs and priorities differ," says Elsa, whose distance with her husband exacerbated because of her husband's health concerns. Though these apps face some skepticism for the developers are just doing business by approaching users' personal lives, some say they are helpful. After all, downloading an app is much more accessible than therapy. Studies have shown that couples may wait for years after they've discovered a problem before seeking counseling. However, the avoided conversation can fester into something much trickier to untangle. Then, such relationship apps that can spark an inspiring conversation and nurture the long-term commitment should be a good solution.

Quiz

( ) 1. According to the article, relationship apps are gaining popularity because _____.
(A) a famous psychologist endorses it
(B) the service fee is rather low
(C) it increases doubt between partners
(D) it sparks meaningful conversations

( ) 2. Why are some people skeptical about the relationship apps?
(A) They are promoted by dating app developers.
(B) The design lacks support of theories.
(C) They are developed for commercial purposes.
(D) They publicize users' personal lives.

( ) 3. Which of the following is NOT mentioned in the article?
(A) The name of the relationship app.
(B) The companies that are developing relationship apps.
(C) How such relationship apps work to help couples.
(D) User's feedback for the apps.

You've probably heard the expression "**opposites**[01] attract." That can be true, but **lasting**[02] relationships are more often built on ____1____ values. Someone who holds the same beliefs you do will ____2____ a better life partner. If you believe in God, ____3____ . If family is a **priority**[03] for you, your partner should also have that priority.

Be especially sure that you agree about money. If the two of you don't, you will have **conflict**[04]. Couples **quarrel**[05] ____4____ money than anything else.

People talk about **love at first sight**[06]. It happens, ____5____ rarely. Making a life-long **commitment**[07] too soon can be a **recipe for disaster**[08]. Give yourself time to really get to know the person first.

Don't spend all your time alone with your special someone. ____6____ , spend time with him or her in lots of different **situations**[09]. Watch how he treats others-and how others respond ____7____ him. You can learn a lot about people ____8____ watching them **interact**[10] with others.

單字片語補充站

01 opposite [形] 相反的　　**06** love at first sight [片] 一見鍾情

02 lasting [形] 持續的　　　**07** commitment [名] 承諾

03 priority [名] 優先考慮的事　**08** recipe for disaster [片] 禍根

04 conflict [名] 衝突　　　　**09** situation [名] 場合、情況

05 quarrel [動] 爭吵　　　　**10** interact [動] 互動

Quiz

( ) **01.** (A) sharing (B) share (C) shared (D) the sharing

( ) **02.** (A) make (B) take (C) do (D) change

( ) **03.** (A) so should your partner (B) so your partner does
(C) so do your partner　　(D) neither does your partner

( ) **04.** (A) more about (B) more (C) even more (D) a lot much

( ) **05.** (A) therefore (B) and (C) however (D) but

( ) **06.** (A) Besides　　　　　(B) Instead
(C) Generally speaking　(D) Furthermore

( ) **07.** (A) to (B) on (C) with (D) for

( ) **08.** (A) in (B) by (C) on (D) before

Adolescents[01] tend to have questions about what healthy dating and romantic relationships should be like. ____1____ They might be influenced by their **peers**[02] or even misled by the **overestimated**[03] hook-up culture. ____2____ It's better for adolescents to learn about the essential **factors**[04] of a healthy relationship. First of all, partners should have **mutual**[05] respect. ____3____ Moreover, romantic partners should have **effective**[06] communication. They should show honesty as well as understanding to each other. Most importantly, partners should come up with solutions to problems effectively. ____4____ What mentioned above are the core **characteristics**[07] of a healthy relationship. Yet, every relationship is **unique**[08]. For adolescents, the focus of relationship should be developing social skills. ____5____ Establishing **positive**[09] social skills during early adolescence may help the young adults develop romantic relationships that are more **exclusive**[10], last longer, and more intimate at later ages.

單字片語補充站

01 adolescent [名] 青少年

02 peer [名] 同儕

03 overestimated [形] 過度強調的

04 factor [名] 因素

05 mutual [形] 互相的

06 effective [形] 有效的

07 characteristic [名] 特色

08 unique [形] 獨特的

09 positive [形] 正向的

10 exclusive [形] 獨佔的

Quiz

(A) The pressure to engage in unhealthy relationship or behaviors may be harmful to teens.

(B) That is, they should be willing to compromise and acknowledge the other person's point of view.

(C) Yet, young adults might not have adequate chances to communicate with adults about this issue.

(D) They should maintain their own individuality while keeping their own friends and hobbies.

(E) There would be more chances to hang out with someone of romantic interest in group settings.

Unit 08-1: 文章概要及重點理解

　　約會應用程式普及的同時，幫助維繫關係的應用程式受歡迎的程度也漸漸增加。這些教導人們「更適當地去愛」的應用程式逐漸成為希望尋求諮商協助夫妻的另類選擇。以「Lasting」這個應用程式為例。這個應用程式是根據相當知名、專攻伴侶關係諮商的心理學家所提供的建議，以及超過三百份夫妻關係的研究結果所設計的。每月付款11.99美元，用戶就會收到通知，要為伴侶做一些小事，像是每天某個時段傳送一封表達感激的簡訊。這個應用程式也會引導用戶去執行比較重要的事，像是開始處理外遇的對話。「這個應用程式就像是兩方都能信任的第三方、中立的中介者，讓我們可以了解我們的需求和優先順序有哪裡不同，」因為她先生健康問題而夫妻關係漸行漸遠的用戶愛紗這樣說道。雖然這類應用程式面臨一些質疑，因為開發者只是為了做生意才去關心個人的生活，但是有些人說這些應用程式是有幫助的。畢竟人下載一個應用程式比尋求治療來得容易許多。研究指出，夫妻常常會在發現問題之後，等很多年才去尋求治療。但是，沒能好好進行的談話會造成更多、更難解決的問題。那麼，這類能促進有效對話並且幫助維繫長期承諾的兩性關係應用程式可能是個好的解決方案。

（ D ）1. 根據這篇文章，兩性關係應用程式會歡迎是因為：
　　　A. 一位知名的心理學家為它代言　　B. 這種服務收費很低
　　　C. 它增加伴侶之間的疑心　　　**D. 它促進有意義的對話。**

（ C ）2. 為什麼有些人會對兩性關係應用程式抱持懷疑態度？
　　　A. 它們是由約會應用程式開發者推薦的。
　　　B. 設計缺乏理論的根據。
　　　C. 它們是為了商業的目的而開發的。
　　　D. 它們會公開用戶的私人生活。

（ B ）3. 下列何者沒有在文章中提到？
　　　A. 兩性關係應用程式的名字。
　　　B. 開發兩性關係應用程式的公司。
　　　C. 這類的應用程式如何有效幫助夫妻。
　　　D. 用戶對這種應用程式的回饋。

Unit **08-2**: 透過克漏字題型強化文法概念

你可能聽說過「異性相吸」這個名詞。這可能是真的，但長久不墜的關係往往建立在共同的價值觀上。與你信仰相同的人會是比較好的人生伴侶。如果你信奉上帝，你的伴侶也當如此。如果你把家庭放在第一位，另一半也應有相同的優先順序。

對金錢的看法特別需要一致，否則就會產生衝突。伴侶們對金錢的爭執往往大於其他事。

人們談到一見鍾情。這是可能發生的，但很少。過於倉促許下一生的承諾可能是不幸的根源。給自己時間先真正的去認識這個人吧！

別把所有時間都放在單獨相處上；反而要花時間和他（她）共度各種不同的場合。注意他如何與別人相處，以及別人如何回應他。觀察人們與別人互動的方式，會對他們有許多了解。

1.C 2.A 3.A 4.A 5.D 6.B 7.A 8.B

Unit **08-3**: 熟悉篇章的前後銜接關係

青少年常會對於健康的約會和感情關係應該是何種樣貌抱持疑問。**(C) 但是，青少年可能不會有足夠的機會和大人溝通這件事。**他們可能會受到同儕的影響或甚至被過度誇大的「勾搭曖昧」文化給誤導。**(A) 這種涉入不健康情感關係或行為的壓力可能會對青少年有不好的影響。**青少年應該要學習健康情感關係的特色。首先，伴侶應該要互相尊重。**(D) 他們應該要維持自己的獨立性，保有自己的朋友和嗜好。**此外，伴侶之間應該要有良好的溝通。他們應該要對彼此誠實並且表示理解。最重要的是，伴侶應該要可以一起有效地找出問題解決方式。**(B) 也就是說，他們應該要願意妥協和認同另一方的觀點。**上述提到的是健康情感關係的核心特質。但是每段關係都是獨特的。對青少年來說，情感關係的焦點應該是發展社會技能。**(E) 應該會有比較多機會可以透過團體活動和喜歡的對象多接觸。**在青少年早期建立正向的社交能力可以幫助青少年在之後的人生階段中發展出比較專一、長久、親密的情感關係。

1.C 2.A 3.D 4.B 5.E

Unit 09-1: 文章概要及重點理解
閱讀全文，並回答下列的問題

Melbourne is in a class of its own. It has been called the world's most livable city. Its three million residents come from all over the world, and their many cultural, religious and racial backgrounds are celebrated in both festivals and day-to-day life. Melbourne is known for its safe and clean environment, its affordable cost of living, and the quality of its housing and education.

Situated on the shores of Port Phillip Bay, at the mouth of the Yarra River, the city has some of the most beautiful parks and tree lined boulevards in the world – all just a few hours away from snow fields and outstanding surfing beaches. The city is well laid out with an extensive network of rail lines, wide and carefully planned roads, bus services and of course, the famous tram network.

Melbourne's climate is excitingly variable, with warm to hot dry summers and cool, crisp, wet winters. Magnificent autumns and springs provide spectacular scenes of changing leaves and blossoms.

All in all, it's easy to describe Melbourne by comparing it to other great cities – London's sophistication, Tokyo's modernity, and Chicago's bold architecture and sculpture all meet in Melbourne's unique approach to life.

( ) 1. Which of the following items is NOT true about Melbourne's climate?

(A) Excitingly changeable.

(B) Cool and dry winter.

(C) Warm to hot dry summer.

(D) Splendid autumn and spring.

( ) 2. When it comes to the traffic, Melbourne does NOT have.

(A) Extensive network of subways.

(B) Bus service.

(C) Tram network.

(D) Carefully planned roads.

( ) 3. Which of the following items is INCORRECT about Melbourne?

(A) Snow fields are just a couple of hours drive from there.

(B) Tree-lined boulevards and parks are both important features.

(C) Deserts add a tropical flavor to Melbourne.

(D) The city is located at the mouth of the Yarra River.

When it comes to the African country Ethiopia, people often think of a **nation**[01] that was ____1____ by **widespread**[02] **starvation**[03] in the 1970s and 1980s. ____2____ this drought-induced famine is ____3____, the country is now striving to **shed**[04] the negative ____4____. In fact, the citizens are **intensely**[05] proud of their status as a nation that was never colonized. ____5____, the rare wolves, **primate**[06] **galore**[07], and exotic cultures make Ethiopia a fascinating destination.

____6____ the political, **infrastructure**[08], and banking challenges for tourists, several friends and I took trip to Ethiopia with a rented ____7____ and a driver. We drove on Africa's highest all-weather road on Sanetti Plateau. Then, we ____8____ an Ethiopian wolf and an **olive baboon**[09] in the Bale Mountains. When visiting Mursi village, we realized that residents in those ____9____ traditional villages aren't as poor as they appear to our Western eyes. The country can present foreign visitors more than ____10____ is shown in a BBC **documentary**[10].

單字片語補充站

01 **nation** [名] 國家

02 **widespread** [形] 廣泛的

03 **starvation** [名] 飢餓

04 **shed** [動] 擺脫

05 **intensely** [副] 強烈地

06 **primate** [名] 靈長類動物

07 **galore** [形] 大量的、許多

08 **infrastructure** [名] 基礎建設

09 **olive baboon** [名] 東非狒狒

10 **documentary** [名] 紀錄片

 Quiz

( ) 01. (A) strike　(B)stroke　(C) struck　(D) stuck

( ) 02. (A) While　(B) Because　(C) Since　(D) Though

( ) 03. (A) undoubted　(B) unbelievable
(C) unthoughtful　(D) undeniable

( ) 04. (A) destination　(B) reputation
(C) regulation　(D) construction

( ) 05. (A) Also　(B) Otherwise(C) However　(D) Therefore

( ) 06. (A) If　(B) Although　(C) In spite　(D) Despite

( ) 07. (A) vehicle　(B) carriage　(C) vessel　(D) aircraft

( ) 08. (A) investigated　(B) detected
(C) spotted　(D) monitored

( ) 09. (A) relevant(B) remote　(C) restricted　(D) realistic

( ) 10. (A) that　(B) which　(C) what　(D) where

The Kingdom of Bhutan is a **landlocked**[01] nation situated between India and China. The entire country is ____1____. The **elevation**[02] gain from the ____2____ . Its traditional **economy**[03] is based on ____3____ . However, these account for less than 50% of the **GDP**[04] now that Bhutan has become an exporter of **hydroelectricity**[05]. Besides, ____4____ .

Bhutan is one of the most **isolated**[06] nations in the world, with **foreign**[07] influences and tourism **regulated**[08] by the government to **preserve**[09] its traditional Tibetan Buddhist culture. It is often **described**[10] as ____5____ .

單字片語補充站

01 landlocked [形] 被陸地包圍的　　**06** isolated [形] 孤立的

02 elevation [名] 海拔、高度　　**07** foreign [形] 國外的

03 economy [名] 經濟　　**08** regulate [動] 管理

04 GDP [名] 國內生產毛額　　**09** preserve [動] 維護
（= Gross Domestic Product）

05 hydroelectricity [名] 水力電氣　　**10** describe [動] 形容、描述

 Quiz

(A) subtropical plains to the glacier-covered Himalayan heights exceeds 7,000m

(B) the last surviving refuge of traditional Himalayan Buddhist culture

(C) forestry, animal husbandry and subsistence agriculture

(D) cash crops and tourism are also significant

(E) mountainous, with the exception of a small strip of ubtropical plains in the extreme south

Unit 09-1: 文章概要及重點理解

墨爾本本身自成一格,被稱為世界上最適合居住的城市。它的三百萬居民來自世界各地,在節慶活動及日常生活中,他們的多種文化、宗教和種族背景都會被慶祝。墨爾本因其安全及乾淨的環境、負擔得起的生活費用和居住及教育的品質而出名。

墨爾本座落於菲律普港灣,也就是在雅拉河河口,該市擁有世上最美的公園及林蔭大道,距離雪地和一流的衝浪海灘只有幾小時的車程而已。該市都市計畫完善,廣泛的鐵路網、寬廣又計劃周詳的馬路和公車服務,當然,也有知名的電車網。

墨爾本的氣候多變頗令人興奮,從溫暖和乾熱的夏天到寒冷、刺骨又潮溼的冬天都有。怡人的春秋兩季帶來百花綻放的壯觀景色。

總之,以比較其它大城市描述墨爾本並不是一件難事—— 一如倫敦的精緻感、東京的現代化,以及芝加哥的大膽建築雕刻,這些特色在墨爾本獨一無二的生活方式中都可看得到。

(B) 1. 談到墨爾本的氣候,哪一項是錯誤的?
  A. 多變頗令人興奮。
  B. 又冷又乾的冬天。
  C. 溫暖和乾熱的夏天。
  D. 怡人的春秋兩季。

(A) 2. 談及交通,墨爾本並沒有下列哪一項?
  A. 廣泛的地鐵網。
  B. 公車服務。
  C. 電車網。
  D. 計劃周詳的馬路。

(C) 3. 關於墨爾本,哪一項是不正確的?
  A. 雪地離這裡開車只需幾小時的車程。
  B. 林蔭大道及公園都是重要的特色。
  C. 沙漠為墨爾本增添了某種熱帶風味。
  D. 該市座落在雅拉河河口。

Unit 09-2: 透過克漏字題型強化文法概念

說到衣索比亞這個非洲國家，人們通常會想到一個在1970和1980年代發生大規模飢荒的國家。雖然這個因乾旱而起的饑荒事件是不可否認的，這個國家還是努力想要擺脫這個負面的名聲。事實上，該國的國民都對於自己國家從未被殖民這件事感到很驕傲。而稀有品種的狼、各種靈長類動物、以及異國的文化，也讓衣索比亞成為一個很吸引人的旅遊勝地。

雖然觀光客可能會遇到在政治、基礎建設、和銀行業務上面遇到一些挑戰，一些朋友和我還是一起包了一台車到衣索比亞旅行。我們開車經過薩內蒂高原上，非洲最高的全天候公路。然後，我們在貝爾山上看到衣索比亞狼和東非狒狒。拜訪摩西部落的時候，我們發現在這個偏遠傳統村莊的居民，其實不像西方人看到的那麼貧窮。來訪者會了解到這個國家與在BBC紀錄片中所呈現內容的不同風貌。

1.C 2.A 3.D 4.B 5.A 6.D 7.A 8.C 9.B 10.C

Unit 09-3: 熟悉篇章的前後銜接關係

不丹王國是個介於印度與中國之間的內陸國家。除了(E)**最南部有一狹長亞熱帶平原外，其餘境內高山林立**。從(A)**亞熱帶平原到滿是冰河覆蓋的喜馬拉雅山這塊區域**，海拔高度超過7,000公尺。不丹王國的傳統經濟仰賴(C)**森林業、畜牧業以及自給自足的農業**。然而，這些僅只佔不到百分之五十的國內生產總值，因為不丹已成為水力發電的輸出國。此外，(D)**經濟作物和觀光業也是很重要的**。

隨著外來的影響以及由政府管理維護傳統藏傳佛教文化的觀光業，不丹是世界最封閉的國家之一。不丹常被形容為(B)**傳統喜馬拉雅佛教文化的最後倖存庇護所**。

1.E 2.A 3.C 4.D 5.B

Everyone may at some point feel under pressure for work-related reasons. Even those who are passionate about their job can experience stressful moments. The stress of meeting a deadline or fulfilling a challenging obligation may sometimes be overwhelming. Such stress may become chronic, which is harmful to both physical and emotional health.

There are some common factors of a stressful workplace, such as low salaries, excessive workloads, and lack of opportunities for promotion. Other job-related stressors include not being granted enough autonomy in professional decisions, or receiving conflicting demands from different stakeholders.

Uncontrolled stress may contribute to health issues, such as insomnia, depression, obesity, heart disease, or weakened immune system. What's more, dealing with stress in unhealthy ways such as overeating, smoking cigarettes, or abusing drugs and alcohol may worsen the problem.

To cope with stress, one can keep track of the situation that creates the most stress. It may be helpful for stress management. Besides, taking time to recharge is essential. Learning some new professional techniques, or relaxing by meditation and deep breathing exercise, would be helpful to reduce the tension and strain at work.

Quiz

( ) 1. **What is the theme of this passage?**
    (A) Politics.
    (B) Entertainment.
    (C) Social News.
    (D) Psychological health.

( ) 2. **What is NOT mentioned in the passage?**
    (A) Suggested reading material for people under pressure.
    (B) Possible reasons of work-related pressure.
    (C) The potential harm of pressure at workplace.
    (D) Useful tips to deal with the job-related pressure.

( ) 3. **The author mentioned that _____ is a proper way to relieve stress.**
    (A) sleeping late on the weekend
    (B) taking professional training courses
    (C) going on a shopping spree
    (D) eating a lot of junk food

Stress is a normal part of life. ____1____ the heavy pressure of modern life, people are more likely to get angry over **trivial**[01] matters. When under stress / pressure, your **attitude**[02] is **extremely**[03] important. It is because if we ____2____ it properly, it can provide the motivation we need to tackle daily challenges and encourage us to try harder when ____3____ difficulties.

Everyone can find their own way to handle the stress as long as he doesn't harm himself. Take myself for example, jogging around the track every day for twenty minutes allows me to **cope with**[04] academic pressure. Recently I have been busy ____4____ for exams, but I am still used to going jogging every Friday after school. After a stressful week, with so many readings and classes, I am always tired of studying. ____5____, I choose to go jogging at the end of the weekdays, so that I can **recharge**[05] my batteries and get ready for **marathon**[06] study sessions on the weekend. If I don't spare some time in jogging, my **efficiency**[07] of study will be reduced. Through jogging, I can turn stress into a **positive force**[08]. That's why I can always be energetic to accept all challenges of life.

單字片語補充站

01 trivial [形] 瑣碎的、不重要的　　**05** recharge [動] 重新充電

02 attitude [名] 態度　　**06** marathon [名] 馬拉松

03 extremely [副] 極度地　　**07** efficiency [名] 效率

04 cope with [片] 處理　　**08** positive force [片] 正面力量

Quiz

( ) **01.** (A) After (B) Above (C) Under (D) Before

( ) **02.** (A) do (B) have (C) are (D) deal with

( ) **03.** (A) face (B) faced (C) facing (D) faces

( ) **04.** (A) prepared (B) prepares (C) prepare (D) preparing

( ) **05.** (A) After all (B) However (C) What's more (D) Therefore

_____1_____ . It is not unusual to hear friends and family members talk about the difficulty they have in managing the stress of everyday life and the **efforts**[01] they make to control the events that cause stress.

Most of us understand the results of not controlling our **reactions**[02] to stress. Forty-three percent of all adults **suffer**[03] terrible health effects from stress. _____2_____ . Stress is **linked**[04] to the six leading causes of death — heart disease, cancer, **lung**[05] disease, accidents, **liver**[06] disease, and **suicide**[07]. _____3_____ .

_____4_____ . Exciting or challenging events like the birth of a child, **completion**[08] of a major project at work, or moving to a new city **generate**[09] as much stress as does **tragedy**[10] or disaster. _____5_____ .

單字片語補充站

01 effort [名] 努力

02 reaction [名] 反應

03 suffer [動] 承受

04 link [動] 連結

05 lung [名] 肺

06 liver [名] 肝

07 suicide [名] 自殺

08 completion [名] 完成

09 generate [動] 引起

10 tragedy [名] 悲劇

Quiz

(A) Most physician office visits are for stress-related illnesses and complaints

(B) And without stress, life would be dull

(C) Currently, health care costs account for about twelve percent of the gross domestic product

(D) Stress has become a favorite subject of everyday conversation

(E) Yet, while stress may damage our health, it is sometimes necessary, even desirable

Unit 10-1: 文章概要及重點理解

　　每個人都有可能會因為工作相關的因素感到壓力。就算是對於工作抱有熱情的人，也有感到壓力的時候。為了趕上期限或者完成一項深具挑戰性的任務，有時會帶來令人無法承受的壓力。有些壓力可能是長期的，可能對身體和心理健康有害。

　　在工作場合有些常見的壓力來源，像是低薪、工作量過大、或者缺乏升遷機會。其他和工作有關的壓力來源包括沒有足夠的專業決定自主權、或者不同利害關係者的要求相衝突等等。

　　壓力沒有處理好，可能會導致一些健康問題，像是失眠、憂鬱、肥胖、心臟疾病、或者免疫系統變弱。更重要的是，用一些不健康的方法來處理壓力，像是大吃大喝、抽煙、或濫用藥物酒精等，會使問題惡化。

　　為了處理壓力，可以紀錄下會造成最多壓力的情境。這可能有助於壓力管理。此外，留一些時間去充實自己也是很重要的。學習一些新的專業技術，或者藉由冥想、深呼吸等方式來放鬆，會有助於減少工作帶來的壓力和緊繃。

(D) 1. 這篇文章的主題為何？

    A. 政治。   B. 娛樂。

    C. 社會新聞。   **D. 心理健康。**

(A) 2. 文章中沒有提到什麼？

    A. 推薦給苦於壓力者的讀物。   B. 工作壓力的可能原因。

    C. 工作壓力可能帶來的傷害。   D. 處理工作壓力的有效方法。

(B) 3. 作者提到＿＿＿＿＿＿是適當的壓力處理方式。

    A. 在週末睡晚一點   **B. 去上專業訓練課程**

    C. 瘋狂購物   D. 吃很多垃圾食物

Unit **10-2:** 透過克漏字題型強化文法概念

壓力是生活中自然的一部份。處在壓力過大的生活環境中，人們變得容易常為小事抓狂。在壓力之下，我們的態度顯得格外的重要。事實上，壓力可以提供處理日常挑戰所需的動機，並鼓勵我們在遇到困難時，去做更努力的嘗試。

只要他不傷害自己，每個人都可以找到自己的方式來面對壓力。舉例來說，天天跑操場二十分鐘，讓我能從課業的壓力中放鬆一下。雖然最近我忙於準備考試，但我還是習慣每週五放學後去慢跑。由於有許多書要讀、不少課要上，在忙碌的一週後，我總是厭倦念書。因此，我選擇在上課日的最後一天去慢跑，這樣我可以重新充電，準備好要在週末進行馬拉松式的讀書計畫。如果我沒有撥些時間慢跑，我讀書的效率便會減低。透過慢跑，我可以把壓力變成正面的力量。這就是為什麼我總是可以充滿活力的接受生活中的所有挑戰。

1.C　2.D　3.C　4.D　5.D

Unit **10-3:** 熟悉篇章的前後銜接關係

(D)壓力已經變成了每天對談中受歡迎的主題。聽見朋友或家庭成員談論他們處理每天生活中壓力的困難以及他們為掌握製造壓力事件所做的努力並不稀奇。

大多數的我們都瞭解不控制我們對壓力的反應會發生什麼後果。43%的成人苦於壓力所造成的嚴重健康影響。(A)大部分到內科診所就診的都是和壓力有關的疾病和抱怨。壓力和六個致死的因素有關連—心臟病、癌症、肺病、意外、肝病和自殺。(C)目前，醫療費用大約佔了國內總消費額的12%。

(E)然而，儘管壓力會傷害我們的健康，但它有時卻是必須的，甚至是令人渴望的。刺激或有挑戰性的事物，像生兒育女、完成一個工作上的重大企畫，或搬到一個新的城市，都會引起悲劇或災難般強烈的壓力。(B)而且，沒有壓力生活多無趣。

1.D　2.A　3.C　4.E　5.B

Unit **11** Languages and Interaction
語言互動篇

Unit **11-1:** 文章概要及重點理解
閱讀全文，並回答下列的問題

A fine way to make friends and introduce yourself to your neighbors in Norway is to present them with a simple gift like a cake or a loaf of bread. Such a gift warms their hearts as well as their stomachs. If you give them expensive gifts, they may become suspicious of your intentions.

If you have never baked a cake before, it may take you months to make a beautiful cake that can stand upright without collapsing. But don't wait for perfection. That moment may never come in this lifetime, and you'll never make any Norwegian friends. Do your best, and when you think your creation is good enough to give away, go for it.

Norwegians are not picky people. They don't demand the best bread from a famous bakery or the most beautiful cake imaginable before they say that you pass the test of friendship. They will appreciate your honest gesture of friendship, even if your bread and cake look…"interesting."

( ) 1. **Present Norwegians with expensive gifts may** _____.
    (A) make them really happy
    (B) arouse their suspicion of your intention
    (C) help you create a firm relationship with them
    (D) scare them away

( ) 2. **How will Norwegians react if they get a cake that looks "interesting"?**
    (A) throw it away immediately
    (B) refuse to eat it
    (C) reject the present
    (D) appreciate the kindness

In your conversations with American adults, you should learn that some topics are safe, but some are not. Work and hobbies are good **starters**[01] for conversations, but ____1____ **avoid**[02] talking about age and money. When you meet an American ____2____ , it is all right for you to ask "What do you do?" Most Americans are happy to talk about it, because they think they are ____3____ by their work. If work does not **prove**[03] to be a productive topic, try other topics ____4____ hobbies. He many get quite excited about a **hobby**[04] he is currently ____5____ with.

The topics of age and money may **rapidly**[05] ____6____ your conversation to an end. Many adult Americans are ____7____ about looking young, so they always keep their age a **secret**[06]. If you carelessly ____8____ this topic, they will often feel quite uneasy or **upset**[07]. **Income**[08] is also a very **sensitive**[09] matter. While Americans may spend a lot of time ____9____ how much other people make, they don't say so. The reason may be that they think people are paid ____10____ their **worth**[10], and they don't want to have their worth known by others.

單字片語補充站

01 **starter** [名] 話題的開端

02 **avoid** [動] 避免

03 **prove** [動] 證明

04 **hobby** [名] 興趣

05 **rapidly** [副] 快速地

06 **secret** [名] 秘密

07 **upset** [形] 不悅的、生氣的

08 **income** [名] 收入

09 **sensitive** [形] 敏感的

10 **worth** [名] 價值

Quiz

( ) **01.** (A) by no means   (B) by all means
       (C) by means of   (D) by any means

( ) **02.** (A) at the first moment   (B) for the first time
       (C) first of all   (D) from the very first

( ) **03.** (A) defined (B) referred (C) controlled (D) proposed

( ) **04.** (A) so as (B) as to (C) as such (D) such as

( ) **05.** (A) involving (B) involve (C) involved (D) involves

( ) **06.** (A) bring (B) let (C) come (D) make

( ) **07.** (A) hasty (B) eager (C) crazy (D) gentle

( ) **08.** (A) touch on (B) put on (C) set on (D) come on

( ) **09.** (A) mastering (B) realizing (C) wondering (D) fulfilling

( ) **10.** (A) appealing to   (B) attending to
       (C) amounting to   (D) according to

It's easier for the human face to smile than **frown**[01]. It takes **twice**[02] as many muscles to frown as it does to smile. Moreover, we do not have to "learn" to do it. ____1____ Children born **blind**[03] never see anybody smile, but they show the same kinds of smiles under the same situations as **sighted**[04] people.

____2____ Some studies **suggest**[05] that the act of shaping our mouths into a smile (creating a **physical**[06] smile) can help us see the brighter, funnier side of things. ____3____ **In addition**[07], smiles **signal**[08] to others that we are people who might be nice to talk to and work with — and that can help us make friends.

____4____ Anything from getting a bad grade on a test to losing an important game can make you feel sad. In such hard times, there seems to be no reason to smile. But there is some good part to almost every bad thing. Turning something that seems all bad into something good is one way to help you smile. ____5____

單字片語補充站

01 frown [動] 皺眉頭　　**05 suggest** [動] 建議

02 twice [形] 兩倍的　　**06 physical** [形] 物理的、身體的

03 blind [形] 瞎的；看不見的　　**07 in addition** [副] 此外

04 sighted [形] 有視力的　　**08 signal** [名] 訊號

Quiz

(A) Smiling is of great help to us.

(B) Although babies imitate the facial expressions they see, smiling isn't just learned by imitation.

(C) Hanging around people who are positive and in good moods is another way to help you find your smile again.

(D) People wearing the physical smile tend to feel happier.

(E) Unfortunately, sometimes you may find it difficult to smile.

Unit **11-1:** 文章概要及重點理解

在挪威，一個交朋友和向鄰居介紹自己的好方法是送他們一個簡單的禮物，像是蛋糕或一條麵包。這樣的禮物溫暖他們的心也溫暖他們的胃。如果你給他們昂貴的禮物，他們可能會懷疑你的動機。

如果你以前從未烤過蛋糕，做出一個可以直立站著不會垮掉的漂亮蛋糕可能會花你幾個月的時間。但別等待完美。這輩子你都等不到那個時候，而且你永遠都不會交到挪威人的朋友。盡力去做，當你覺得你的作品好到可以給人時，就給吧。

挪威人不挑剔。他們不會要求有名麵包坊的頂級麵包或想像得到的最漂亮的蛋糕才説你通過了友情試煉。他們會賞識你坦率的友誼之舉，即使你的麵包和蛋糕看起來有點……有趣。

（ B ）1. 送昂貴的禮物給挪威人，可能會 ＿＿＿＿＿＿＿ 。
(A) 使他們非常開心
(B) 懷疑你的動機
(C) 幫助你建立一個堅固的友誼
(D) 把他們嚇跑

（ D ）2. 當他們收到了看起來「很有趣」的蛋糕時，他們可能會如何反應？
(A) 馬上丟掉
(B) 拒絕吃掉
(C) 拒絕收下
(D) 感謝好意

Unit **11-2:** 透過克漏字題型強化文法概念

當你和美國的成年人聊天時，你應該要知道，有些話題很安全，有些話題則不。工作和興趣常是一個話題的好開端，但一定要想辦法避免談論年紀和金錢。當你第一次遇到一個美國人時，詢問他的職業是沒有問題的。大多數美國人樂於談論此話題，因為他們認為他們的工作能勾勒出他們自己的樣子。如果工作這個話題不能讓對方侃侃而談，試著談論其他話題，像是興趣。他可能會在談論他最近熱衷的某個興趣時變得興奮不已。

年紀和金錢的話題會急速為你們的談話劃下句點。許多成年美國人著迷於使自己看起來年輕，所以他們總是將年齡當作秘密。如果你粗心地觸及這一主題，他們常會覺得不適或不快。收入也是一個非常敏感的話題。儘管美國人可能會花許多時間想其他人賺了多少錢，他們自己卻不會透露。原因可能是因為他們覺得人的薪水多寡根據的是人的價值，而他們不想讓別人知道他們的價值。

1.B　2.B　3.A　4.D　5.C　6.A　7.C　8.A　9.C　10.D

Unit **11-3: 熟悉篇章的前後銜接關係**

對人的臉來說，微笑比皺眉容易。皺眉要運用到微笑時兩倍的肌肉。除此之外，我們不用學如何去微笑。**(B)儘管嬰兒會模仿他們見到的表情，微笑卻不是由模仿學來的。**生下來就看不見的小孩從來沒見過任何人笑，但他們能露出和一般小孩一樣的微笑。

(A)微笑對我們大有幫助。有些研究顯示，將我們的嘴巴做出微笑的動作（做出一個肉體上的微笑）可以幫助我們看到事物較為有趣與光明的一面。**(D)有著微笑的人們傾向於感到更快樂。**此外，微笑能向其他人發出訊號，顯示我們是能交談和一起工作的好夥伴，有助於結交朋友。

(E)遺憾的是，有時候你會發現微笑很難。從考試的爛成績到輸掉一場重要的比賽都會使你感到傷心。在艱難的時候，好像沒有微笑的理由。但幾乎每個壞事都有一些好的層面。將一件全部是壞的事想成某種好事是一個幫助你微笑的好方法。**(C)而多和正面和擁有好心情的人在一起是另一個幫助你找回微笑的好方法。**

1.B　2.A　3.D　4.E　5.C

Unit 12-1: 文章概要及重點理解
閱讀全文，並回答下列的問題

In Taiwan, typhoons usually come in summer. They bring strong wind and lots of rainfall. The weather bureau will warn us one or two days before they come. You can see people doing such things as cutting down tall trees and fixing their houses.

However, when typhoons come, we can do nothing but wait for their passing away. You will see trees falling down and houses without roofs. In the country, crops are deep in the muddy water. Water is everywhere. Fish swim on the highways and in the fields. Transportation has to stop. Some careless drivers even drive their cars into ditches when hurrying home.

In such weather conditions, people have to stay at home. Inside the house children get bored, so some of them go out to catch fish on the highways or fight water battles in spite of the strong wind and heavy rain.

Although typhoons are common in Taiwan and we have got used to them, I believe no one likes them.

( ) 1. **In Taiwan, typhoons usually come in** _____.

   (A) spring

   (B) summer

   (C) fall

   (D) winter

( ) 2. **Before typhoons come, people cut down tall trees because** _____.

   (A) they need shades no more

   (B) the tall trees will block their view

   (C) they need wood to make fires

   (D) the tall trees may bring more damage when they fall down in the strong wind

( ) 3. **During the typhoon,** _____.

   (A) drivers are safe on the highways

   (B) transportation has to stop

   (C) there will be a terrible drought

   (D) children like to stay at home

Volcanic ____1____ is an awesome demonstration of nature's power. It happens when **magma**[01], rock in **molten**[02] or melted form, approaches the surface of the earth along **chimney-like**[03] channels or **vents**[04]. The vent is sometimes **clogged**[05] because the magma is relatively cool, thick, and slow moving. Under these circumstances, the gas and steam ____2____ in the magma cannot separate out easily. They form bubbles within the magma. At some point, pressure from the **accumulations**[06] of these bubbles then becomes so great ____3____ the volcano explodes.

Such violent eruptions can have many ____4____, including rapidly moving clouds of extremely hot gas and ash, great sea waves, **mudflows**[07], brilliant sunsets, and forest fires. ____5____ the location of the volcano, the effect on human lives can be devastating. The ancient city of Pompeii was completely destroyed when Mt. Vesuvius ____6____ in 79 A.D. Without **warning**[08], the city's twenty thousand inhabitants were buried in volcanic ash and hot mud. The once thriving city ____7____ from view until **excavated**[09] by **archeologists**[10] in the 18th century.

單字片語補充站

01 **magma** [名] 岩漿	**06** **accumulation** [名] 堆積
02 **molten** [形] 熔化的	**07** **mudflow** [名] 岩石流
03 **chimney-like** [形] 煙囪形的	**08** **warning** [名] 警告
04 **vent** [名] 火山口、排氣孔	**09** **excavate** [動] 挖掘
05 **clog** [動] 阻塞	**10** **archeologist** [名] 考古學家

Quiz

( ) **01.** (A) interruption (B) disruption (C) eruption (D) intersection

( ) **02.** (A) contained (B) contain (C) are contained (D) that contain

( ) **03.** (A) therefore (B) thus (C) that (D) as a result

( ) **04.** (A) affects (B) affections (C) forms (D) causes

( ) **05.** (A) Depend on (B) Depended upon
(C) Depend (D) Depending on

( ) **06.** (A) erupt (B) eruption (C) erupted (D) was erupted

( ) **07.** (A) disappeared (B) disappearing
(C) to disappear (D) has disappeared

In October, 2019, Hagibis struck Japan and dumped more than three feet of rain, shattering the country's **rainfall** [01] record. ____1____ Two other storms were expected to hit the **archipelago** [02] nation back-to-back. ____2____ The tropical rainstorm **lashed** [03] Japan with heavy downpour and **gusty** [04] winds. It was later downgraded and reclassified as an **extratropical** [05] cyclone by the Japan **Meteorological** [06] Agency. ____3____ It poured 3 to 7 inches of rain in southern Japan. After it came Bualoi, a typhoon that went through a period of rapid **intensification** [07] near Guam. ____4____ However, the heavy rain it brought increase the risk of flooding. The local government was forced to put off **reconstruction** [08] work after Hagibis. Residents are now working to restore normal life after the consecutive storms wreaked havoc the island country. ____5____ Meteorologists called for more efforts to predict the coverage of **torrential** [09] band. Also, the warning system for **evacuation** [10] should be upgraded so that more people can take shelter in time.

單字片語補充站

01 **rainfall** [名] 降雨量

02 **archipelago** [名] 群島

03 **lash** [動] 打擊

04 **gusty** [形] 強風的

05 **extratropical** [形] 溫帶的

06 **meteorological** [形] 氣象學家

07 **intensification** [名] 強化

08 **reconstruction** [名] 重建

09 **torrential** [形] 滂沱的

10 **evacuation** [名] 撤離

 **Quiz**

(A) Some measures should be taken to improve the efficiency disaster prevention and reconstruction.

(B) First up was Neoguri, which was initially identified a Category 2-equivalent typhoon.

(C) However, Neoguri remained a potent system.

(D) After the devastating typhoon, the region faced threats of flooding and landslide again.

(E) It turned out that typhoon Bualoi did not strike the mainland of Japan.

Unit **12-1**: 文章概要及重點理解

颱風經常在夏天侵襲臺灣，帶來強風和豐沛的雨量。颱風來臨之前，氣象局會預先發佈颱風警報，這個時候，可以看到民眾進行砍大樹、維修房屋等防颱措施。

然而颱風來時，我們就只能待在家裡等著它過境。你會目睹樹倒了，房子的屋頂被吹走了。在鄉間，農作物則深陷泥沼中。到處都淹水，魚兒在公路上或田間游來游去，交通因而中斷。而一些粗心大意的駕駛朋友因為急著回家，甚至把車子開進水溝。

人們在這種天氣下，不得不待在家裡，孩子們在屋子裡悶的發慌，於是有些小孩不顧狂風暴雨，跑到馬路上去捉魚或是打起水仗來。

雖然在台灣颱風很普遍，而我們也已經習以為常，但我相信沒有人喜歡颱風。

(B) 1. 在台灣颱風通常在_____時來到。
　　　A. 春天　　　　　　　　　　B. **夏天**
　　　C. 秋天　　　　　　　　　　D. 冬天

(D) 2. 在颱風來臨前，人們砍斷大樹是因為？
　　　A. 他們不再需要陰影
　　　B. 高的樹會擋住他們的視線
　　　C. 他們需要生火的木材
　　　D. **高的樹在強風中倒下時會帶來更大的傷害**

(B) 4. 颱風時，_____。
　　　A. 駕駛在馬路上很安全　　　B. **必須中斷交通系統**
　　　C. 會發生嚴重的乾旱　　　　D. 小孩子喜歡待在家裡

Unit **12-2**: 透過克漏字題型強化文法概念

火山爆發是自然力量的驚人展示。它在岩漿（岩石在熔化或軟化時的形式）沿著煙囪形的通道靠近地表或是火山口時發生。火山口有時候被堵塞，因為岩漿的溫度相對低、濃稠而且移動緩慢。在這樣的條件下，岩漿中的氣體和蒸氣無法輕易地分離。他們在岩漿中形成泡沫。在某個時刻，由於這些泡沫的累積極大形成壓力，便造成火山爆發。

像這樣猛烈的爆發有許多影響，像是快速移動的極熱氣體和火山灰的雲、大海嘯、泥石流、燦爛的日落及森林大火。隨著火山位置的不同，對於人類的影響可能是毀滅性的。當維蘇威火山在公元79年爆發時，古城市龐貝被完全摧毀。城市的二萬名居民在毫無預警的情況下被活埋在火山灰和熱泥之中。一度繁榮的城市消失在人們眼前，直到十八世紀考古學家將它挖掘出來。

1.C　2.A　3.C　4.B　5.D　6.C　7.A

Unit **10-3**: 熟悉篇章的前後銜接關係

在2019年十月，海貝思颱風襲擊日本，帶來三英尺的雨量，刷新的了日本的雨量紀錄。**(D) 在這次颱風摧殘之後，這個地區又再度面臨淹水和山崩的危機。又有兩個颱風可能要接連著襲擊這個群島國家。(B) 首先是颱風浣熊，它一開始被認定是一個強度等同於第二類颱風的颱風。**這個熱帶風暴襲擊日本，帶來暴雨和強風。它後來強度減弱，被日本氣象局重新歸類為溫帶氣漩。**(C) 然而，颱風浣熊還是一個結構堅強的風暴系統。**它為日本南部帶來三到七英吋的雨量。接著是颱風博羅依，這個颱風在關島附近快速增強。**(E) 最後颱風博羅依沒有襲擊日本本土。**但是，它所帶來的豪雨還是增加了淹水的風險。當地政府被迫中斷海貝絲颱風之後的重建工作。居民正在努力在接連的颱風摧殘之後，讓生活回到正軌。**(A) 有關當局應該要採取一些措施來增加防災以及重建的效率。**氣象學家呼籲要投入更多心力在預測豪雨帶範圍。此外，應該要升級警示系統，幫助人們及時避難。

1.D　2.B　3.C　4.E　5.A

Knowledge of Technology
科技知識篇

Unit 13-1: 文章概要及重點理解
閱讀全文，並回答下列的問題

Spotify is uncontestably the king of music streaming. It is a Swedish firm founded in 2006. The founders, Ek and Martin Lorentzon, started up the company in the conventional Stockholm suburb. The platform has been streaming the most popular music from Madonna to Daft Punk. Over the course of the years, the company has distributed over millions of songs and accumulated over 71 million paying customers worldwide.

The company's business is more than twice the size of its closest rival, Apple Music. Other competitors include Google Music, Tidal, Deezer, and Napster. Despite its estimated value of as much as $23.4 billion, the company has yet to turn a profit. Even with its application to list some of its existing share on the New York Stock Exchange, the situation seemed far from optimistic. The condition was better after it allied with Facebook and launched service in the U.S. in 2011.

In the document filed to the US stock market regulator, the chief executive and co-founder Danial Ek claim the company "would improve the world, one song at a time." Despite the creators' vision, Spotify has been facing some concerns. For one thing, though the company survived the transition from vinyl to cassettes to CDs, but it's slow to release the app written for smartphones. On the other hand, top artists complained that the streaming service might cannibalize sales of their albums. The company has a glorious past may have to endure bumpy ride.

Quiz

( ) 1. **What was NOT mentioned about Spotify in the passage?**
   (A) The number of its users.
   (B) Its business size.
   (C) The company's value.
   (D) The monthly subscription fees.

( ) 2. **Spotify collaborated with _____ in exploring the U.S. markets.**
   (A) Facebook   (B) Google
   (C) Napster   (D) Apple

( ) 3. **The aim of "improving the world one song at a time" was mentioned by _____.**
   (A) Madonna
   (B) Daft Punk
   (C) Danial Ek
   (D) Martin Lorentzon

Though it may be hard to believe, **optical illusion**[01] can be used to make road safer. This rather strange fact was first discovered in Japan. The Japanese decided to ____1____ with certain patterns painted on the **surface**[02] of road to see if they could fool drivers into slowing down. The experiment was a **resounding**[03] success. As it ____2____ , the **bent**[04] stripes heightened the sense of speed drivers felt, with the result that they actually slowed down. The effect was so ____3____ that the accident rate on some roads was cut by 75 percent.

With results like that it wasn't long before other countries ____4____ notice. Plans are already ____5____ in the US to try and repeat or perhaps even improve upon Japan's success. Chevrons (angled stripes) and **patterns**[05] will be painted on roads around the country ____6____ to find out which work best under what **conditions**[06]. ____7____ the fact that speeding plays a role in as many 20 percent of all **fatal**[07] traffic accidents, this simple and **relatively**[08] inexpensive method of getting drivers to slow down has the ____8____ to save thousands of lives each year.

單字片語補充站

01 optical illusion [名] 光學幻象
02 surface [名] 表面
03 resounding [形] 令人注目的、迴響的
04 bent [形] 彎折的
05 pattern [名] 圖樣
06 condition [名] 條件
07 fatal [形] 致命的
08 relatively [副] 相對而言

Quiz

( ) **01.** (A) test   (B) experiment   (C) try   (D) implement

( ) **02.** (A) turned out (B) went through
　　　(C) worked up (D) resulted from

( ) **03.** (A) minute (B) diverse (C) pronounced (D) vague

( ) **04.** (A) should   (B) go   (C) had   (D) took

( ) **05.** (A) carrying out (B) underway (C) forwarding (D) motivated

( ) **06.** (A) in an effort (B) along the way
　　　(C) in the manner (D) by such means

( ) **07.** (A) Since (B) Although (C) Given (D) Following

( ) **08.** (A) record (B) prediction (C) potential (D) intention

Unit 13-3: 熟悉篇章的前後銜接關係
閱讀全文，並選出空格中該填入的句

The idea of creating a **cryptocurrency**[01] may seem unrealistic. To Facebook, however, it is an inevitable trend. ____1____ In fact, the company has ambitious plan to replace traditional money with the Libra, its self-developed cryptocurrency.

The Libra project has been incubated for over a year. **Initially**[02], 27 partners took part in it, which could have helped to **legitimize**[03] and spread the cryptocurrency. ____2____ The project has also been **dismissed**[04] as impractical by **regulators**[05] and lawmakers. The company's hand-off **stance**[06] towards fake political advertising and Cambridge Analytica data **scandal**[07] also made many users lose faith in it.

____3____ Mr. Zuckerberg has **testified**[08] at the House Financial Service Committee that the company has ability to protect users' data. David Marcus, the head of Libra project, also **delivered**[09] a speech at World Bank and a meeting of the Group of 30. ____4____ Unfortunately, these efforts might not have removed the doubt on digital money. It didn't get support from the government, either. ____5____ The Libra Project is expected to face many challenges before it could be actually **launched**[10].

單字片語補充站

01 cryptocurrency [名] 加密貨幣

02 initially [副] 起初

03 legitimize [動] 合法化

04 dismiss [動] 不予理會

05 regulator [名] 管理者、監管者

06 stance [名] 立場

07 scandal [名] 醜聞

08 testify [動] 證詞

09 deliver [動] 發表

10 launch [動] 發行、啟動

 Quiz

(A) The company's executives have been expending a lot of efforts in defending the cryptocurrency plan.

(B) Yet, key partners like Visa and Mastercard have withdrawn from it.

(C) Its CEO, Mr. Zuckerberg has aspired to make digital coins line Bitcoin.

(D) He hoped to win support from global leaders.

(E) The U.S. political system seems to be willing to turn its back on this technological innovation.

Answer 中文翻譯及參考解答

Unit **13-1**: 文章概要及重點理解

　　Spotify 毫無疑問是傳流音樂界的龍頭老大。它是一間在2006年創立的瑞典公司。創辦人丹尼爾·埃克和馬丁·羅倫佐是在保守的斯德哥爾摩近郊創立這間公司。這個平台串流的音樂從瑪丹娜到傻瓜龐克的歌都有。在過去幾年的發展中，該公司已經發布了好幾百首歌曲，並且在全球累積了超過七千一百萬名的付費用戶。

　　這間公司的商業規模比實力最接近的對手Apple Music還要大兩倍。其他還有一些競爭對手包括Google Music、Tidal、Deezer、以及Napster。儘管它的市值估計有234億，這間公司卻還未能獲利。即使申請於紐約股市公開發行公司現有的股票，情況仍不樂觀。一直到2011年，公司和Facebook合作開始於美國推行這項服務，情況才好轉。

　　根據紐約股市主管機關的一份文件，執行長及公司共同創辦人丹尼爾·埃克宣稱公司會「一次一首歌地改變世界」。儘管公司有這樣的願景，Spotify還是面臨了一些困境。首先，雖然公司撐過了黑膠、卡帶、一直到CD的轉變，卻在發行智慧型手機應用程式這方面動作太慢。另外，知名藝人抱怨這種串流音樂服務減少了他們的唱片銷售量。儘管這間公司有著光榮的過去，未來可能也會有辛苦的路要走。

(D) 1. 文章中沒有提到有關Spotify的哪一件事？
　　　A. 用戶的人數　　　　　　　B. 生意的規模
　　　C. 公司的市值　　　　　　　**D. 每月的收費**

(A) 2. Spotify 和_____合作以開發美國市場。
　　　A. Facebook　　　　　　　B. Google
　　　C. Napster　　　　　　　　　D. Apple

(C) 3.「一次一首歌地改變世界」這個願景是由_____提出的。
　　　A. 瑪丹娜　　　　　　　　　B. 傻瓜龐克
　　　C. 丹尼爾·埃克　　　　　　D. 馬丁·羅倫佐

Unit **13-2**: 透過克漏字題型強化文法概念

　　雖然聽起來難以相信，光學幻象可以被用來使得道路更為安全。這個頗為奇特的事實首先於日本被發現。日本人決定在道路表面上油漆特定的圖案來實驗，想看看這樣能不能欺騙駕駛人讓他們減速。實驗室轟動一時的成功，結果顯示彎折的線條增加了駕駛人的速度感，造成駕駛人真的會減低速度。其效果是如此地顯著，以致於某些道路發生意外的比例下降了百分之七十五。

不久之後這樣的結果使其他國家開始注意。美國已經計劃嘗試複製日本成功的經驗，甚至於利用成功的經驗進一步改善。有角度的線條和其它圖樣將在全國各地的道路上繪製，以期發現在何種狀況之下的效果最佳。當速度在所有致命的交通意外裡扮演達到百分之二十角色的前提之下，這樣簡單而且相對便宜能讓駕駛人減速的方法的確具有拯救數以千計生命的潛力。

1.B　2.A　3.C　4.D　5.B　6.A　7.C　8.C

Unit **13-3: 熟悉篇章的前後銜接關係**

創造出一個日常生活中使用的加密貨幣似乎是一件不太實際的事情。但是對Facebook公司來說，這是不可避免的趨勢。**(C) 該公司的總裁佐克伯先生立志要創造一個像比特幣一樣的電子貨幣。**事實上，該公司有一項雄心壯志的計畫，是要用他們自行研發的加密貨幣Libra取代傳統的貨幣。

Libra計畫已經醞釀超過一年了。起初，有27位夥伴加入，幫助合法化和廣泛使用這個加密貨幣。**(B) 但是Visa和 Mastercard 等重要合作夥伴已退出計畫。**這個計畫也被金融監管者和立法者認為是不通的。該公司對於假政治廣告以及劍橋分析資料外洩的醜聞漠不關心的態度，也使許多用戶對該公司失去信心。

(A) 公司的執行長們一直努力維護這個加密貨幣計畫。佐克伯先生對聯邦眾議院金融服務委員會發表證詞，說明公司會等到Libra計畫獲得批准才會發行。Libra計畫的負責人，大衛·馬可斯，也在一個世界銀行的三十國會議上發表演說。**(D) 他希望可以獲得全球領袖的支持。**然而，這些努力可能無法消弭對電子或地的疑慮。它也未能得到美國政府的支持。**(E) 美國的政治體系似乎不太贊同這項科技創新。**Libra計畫真正啟動之前，可能還需要面臨不少挑戰。

1.C　2.B　3.A　4.D　5.E

 Unit **14-1:** 文章概要及重點理解
閱讀全文，並回答下列的問題

In the United States, there are certain social events at which a hot dog is almost the only acceptable food — at circuses, picnics, fairs, and so on. It has also become indispensable at a sports event. It is estimated that sixty percent of the people who attend sports events will eat at least one hot dog during the game. If the home team takes a comfortable lead, hot dog sales are brisk, but if the game is close, hot dog sales decline.

Connoisseurs say that a good hot dog should be beefy and crispy. They want to hear a little pop and get a spurt of juice when they bite into a hot dog, which calls for natural casing, preferably sheep. But most hot dogs now sold in the United States are skinless. The good news is that there is a relatively new edible casing fabricated from beef collagen (a gelatin-like protein). To hot dog connoisseurs, though, nothing tastes the same as sheep casing.

( ) 1. **From the passage, what can be inferred about hot dogs in the United States?**
(A) Americans eat more hot dogs than any other people.
(B) Americans like hot dogs at a variety of events.
(C) Most hot dogs taste the same.
(D) Hot dogs usually have a crispy skin.

( ) 2. **At a sports event, what happens when the home team is ahead by a large margin?**
(A) Hot dog sales decline.
(B) People eat more hot dogs.
(C) Hot dog sales remain constant.
(D) People demand crisper hot dogs.

( ) 3. **From the passage, what can be inferred about hot dog connoisseurs?**
(A) They like skinless hot dogs.
(B) They will not eat hot dogs in sheep casing.
(C) They feel that the new collagen casings are better than sheep casings.
(D) The notice a difference between the new collagen casings and sheep casings.

Humans around the world eat a **wide**[01] ____1____ of plants and animals. Take hot chili peppers for example. About one-fourth of the world's **population**[02] ____2____ them regularly. South American Indians ate them 9000 years ago. Columbus first ____3____ them to **Spain**[03], and now they **grow**[04] and are eaten in most ____4____ parts of the world, like South America, many parts of North America, and Asia.

Why do so many people eat **chili peppers**[05]? Chili peppers **contain**[06] ____5____ **vitamins**[07] that help the body grow and stay healthy. They can also make you sweat; this ____6____ in hot weather. Eventually, some scientists are ____7____ that chili peppers can help ____8____ food in hot weather.

What don't people eat? Most North Americans and Europeans, for example, don't eat **insects**[08]. ____9____ will they eat dogs and cats. They do, however, eat pork, whereas about one-third of the world's population won't eat pork. Furthermore, North Americans and Europeans eat huge numbers of ____10____ products, while people in a number of cultures do not. Some of these cultures won't have milk as food – they simply make cheese or butter of it instead.

單字片語補充站

01 **wide** [形] 寬闊的、廣泛的　　**05** **chili pepper** [名] 辣椒

02 **population** [名] 人口　　　　**06** **contain** [動] 含有

03 **Spain** [名] 西班牙　　　　　**07** **vitamin** [名] 維他命

04 **grow** [動] 種植　　　　　　　**08** **insect** [名] 昆蟲

Quiz

( ) **01.** (A) variety (B) various (C) varsity (D) vary

( ) **02.** (A) using (B) is using (C) use (D) uses

( ) **03.** (A) bringing (B) brings (C) bought (D) brought

( ) **04.** (A) cool (B) infertile (C) warm (D) fecund

( ) **05.** (A) many great　　　(B) great much
　　　　(C) a great many　　(D) a plenty of

( ) **06.** (A) keep your cool　　(B) make you chilly
　　　　(C) calm you down　　(D) cools you off

( ) **07.** (A) doubtful (B) convinced (C) believed (D) persuaded

( ) **08.** (A) preserved (B) preserve (C) preserving (D) to preserve

( ) **09.** (A) Likewise (B) Nor (C) Neither (D) Either

( ) **10.** (A) daisy (B) dairy (C) diary (D) daily

Mention "McDonald's" to any child and you will **definitely**[01] see his eyes light up. ____1____ . This fast-food restaurant, which has taken the world by storm, was **pioneered**[02] by Mr. Richard McDonald and his brother, Maurice. ____2____ .

In 1940, the two brothers started a barbecue restaurant at a carpark selling hot dogs. ____3____ . After World War II, the McDonald's opened a self-service **drivethrough**[03] restaurant selling hamburgers and French fries.

After some years, they eventually **granted**[04] the **exclusive**[05] **franchise**[06] rights to Ray Kroc, who formed the company franchising the whole business operation **worldwide**[07]. ____4____ .

However, it must be noted that it was Richard McDonald who first **sketched**[08] the golden **arches**[09] of the letter "M", grilled the first McDonald hamburger, and designed the **thermometer**[10] used to ensure that food at McDonald's is always cooked at the right temperature. ____5____ .

單字片語補充站

01 definitely [副] 肯定

02 pioneer [動] 開闢、開拓

03 drive-through [名] 得來速

04 grant [動] 授權

05 exclusive [形] 獨家的

06 franchise [名] 特權、經銷權

07 worldwide [形] 遍及全球的

08 sketch [動] 勾勒

09 arch [名] 弧形、拱形

10 thermometer [名] 溫度計

 Quiz

(A) People used to love their hot dogs and would eat them in their cars

(B) He died at the age of 89 in July 1998

(C) Little did they know that it would one day turn into a multibillion dollar business

(D) It became the most successful food service organization in the world

(E) Children just cannot resist its food and free-gifts

Unit 14-1: 文章概要及重點理解

在美國有某些社交場合，熱狗幾乎是唯一受人歡迎的食品——如看馬戲、野餐、展覽會等等。在運動會時熱狗已成為不可或缺的食品。據估計參加運動會的人，有百分之六十會在會場裡至少吃一個熱狗。如果地主隊分數遙遙領先，熱狗生意興隆，但是假如雙方比數很接近，熱狗生意則一落千丈。

美食專家說好熱狗應該多肉而脆。當他們一口咬下去的時候，希望聽到輕輕噗的一聲而且嚐到迸湧而出的肉汁，這種熱狗就需要天然的外皮，最好是羊腸，然而目前美國出售的熱狗多半是沒皮的。好消息是，最近出現了一種新的可食外皮，由牛骨膠質（一種類似膠狀的蛋白質）製成。不過對於熱狗的行家而言，沒有東西味道比得上羊腸。

（ B ）1. 由本文可推知什麼有關美國熱狗的事情？
A. 美國人吃熱狗比其他人要多。　B. 美國人喜歡在各種場合吃熱狗。
C. 多數的熱狗味道相同。　　　　D. 熱狗通常有一層脆皮。

（ B ）2. 運動會時，當地主隊分數領先很多時，會發生什麼事情？
A. 熱狗生意一落千。　　　　　　B. 人們吃更多的熱狗。
C. 熱狗生意保持不斷。　　　　　D. 人們要求更脆的熱狗。

（ D ）3. 由本文可推知什麼有關熱狗行家的事情？
A. 他們喜歡無皮的熱狗。
B. 他們不會吃羊腸外皮的熱狗。
C. 他們感覺新出的膠質外皮比羊腸外皮好吃。
D. 他們注意到新出的膠質外皮的羊腸外皮的不同。

Unit 14-2: 透過克漏字題型強化文法概念

全世界的人們所吃的動植物都很不相同，就拿辣椒來說吧，全世界大約四分之一的人固定使用它為食。南美洲的印地安人早在9000年前就以辣椒為食了，哥倫布將它引入西班牙，而現在在世界上溫暖的地區都有人種植和食用，比如南美、北美大部分地區、亞洲。

為什麼這麼多人吃辣椒呢？辣椒有大量的維他命可以幫助身體成長和保持健康。而且辣椒可以讓你流汗，讓你在熱天時覺得涼快一點。最後，有科學家深信辣椒可以讓食物在熱天中不易腐壞。

那有什麼食物是人類不吃的呢？舉例來説，大部分的北美洲和歐洲的人不吃昆蟲，他們也不吃狗，也不吃貓，可是，他們常吃豬肉，而全世界有三分之一的人是不吃豬肉的。而且，北美洲和歐洲的人吃很多乳製品，而很多其他文化的人們是不吃的，在有些文化當中的人不喝牛奶，不過他們把牛奶做成乳酪或奶油食用。

1.A　2.D　3.D　4.C　5.C　6.D　7.B　8.B　9.C　10.B

Unit 14-3: 熟悉篇章的前後銜接關係

你只要向任何小孩提到「麥當勞」，肯定會看到他的眼睛為之一亮。**(E)孩子們就是無法抗拒麥當勞的食物以及免費的禮物。**這家速食餐廳，像一陣暴風般地席捲整個世界。它的開山始祖是理查麥當勞及其弟弟莫理斯麥當勞。**(C)他們沒想到有一天這家速食餐廳會轉變成億萬美元的大企業。**

一九四〇年，這對兄弟在某汽車公園裡開了一家烤肉餐廳賣熱狗。**(A)大家很喜歡這些熱狗，買了之後會在車子裡享用。**二次大戰後，麥氏兄弟開了一家自助得來速餐廳賣漢堡及薯條。

若干年後，他們終於將連鎖店的加盟權給予雷克羅克，於是克羅克就組了公司，在世界各地開展連鎖企業，**(D)並成了全世界最成功的食品業公司。**

不過，有一點要提的是理查麥當勞是最早勾畫出金黃色弧形，也就是M這個字母的人，他也是最早烤出一份麥當勞漢堡的人，同時又設計出一種溫度計，可以確保麥當勞的食品始終都是以標準的溫度烘烤的。(B)他於一九九八年七月過世，享年八十九歲。

1.E　2.C　3.A　4.D　5.B

Those who are involved in a cross-cultural relationship may sometimes feel overwhelmed by a myriad of problems. However, couples and families can take heart from the following suggestions. The social, physical, and relationship issues of interracial marriage and family have some effective solutions.

Dialogue is important in all kinds of relationships. Married couples coming from different cultures may need to pay even more efforts in communicating and accommodating each other. Interracial couples need to speak candidly about what is acceptable rule of cleanliness, distribution of tasks to spouses, ways to raise kids, and guidelines in disciplining the kids.

The differences in language, custom, and religious beliefs in an intercultural family may bring about some challenges. However, kids in such family can actually benefit from such background. First, children can spontaneously learn to be multi-lingual in the early stage of development.

Also, they could learn to be more tolerant to different religious beliefs and practices. With positive attitude, the intercultural marriage can help the family to embark on a wonderful journey of discovery and happiness.

( ) 1. What is the theme of this article?
(A) Sociology.
(B) Geography.
(C) Politics.
(D) Meteorology.

( ) 2. What is NOT mentioned as a potential problem of interracial marriage?
(A) The kids may be forced to separate from one of the parents.
(B) The couple may have different religious beliefs.
(C) Parents may have different ideas about how to educate the children.
(D) The language barrier may make communication more challenging.

( ) 3. According to the article, children can benefit from the intercultural family background as long as their parents _____.
(A) seek social support
(B) actively participate in community activities
(C) change their customs and beliefs
(D) can be openminded and tolerant

Five years ago, Eric met Jennifer for the first time at a party. At that very moment, Eric wanted to ____1____ the pretty girl with big eyes after the party came to an end. Three months later, ____2____ several times, they fell in love with each other. They had **cheeked by jowl**[01] for months. Eric decided to propose to his loved one, Jennifer, who was 23 years old. They got engaged, married on the same date, when Eric was 28. Since they spent a wonderful honeymoon, ____3____ the town red almost all night long, Jennifer was pregnant.

After ten months, she ____4____ a baby girl named Lisa, like her mother who was with brilliant eyes. But during the period of the time, Jennifer nearly every morning got out on the wrong side of bed owing to the symptom of being pregnant. At first, Eric was considerate, ____5____ Jennifer's **running amuck**[02]. But later, Eric had affairs with other girls to release his mood. Worst of all, he often stayed outside, leaving his loved wife alone home.

They started to have a big fight when Eric was home. The situation was like their living separately. One night, two weeks before Lisa came to the world, Jennifer can't help bursting out crying and trying to **call Eric's bluff**[03]. She almost lost her temper and kept on yelling at Eric, but in vain. Eric seemed not to **bury the hatchet**[04], looking at Jennifer coldly with a smile. Poor Jennifer, who was helpless then, couldn't recognize the man ____6____ in the front of her. All of the happy hours they ____7____ fast passed by her mind, her heart was totally broken. The only thing she cared about was how to live on with her single parent baby. So she turned to Eric, begging him to give both of the girls a break. But the iron-hearted man just walked away. Having gone through the two-week dark, lonely, and hopeless lives, Jennifer determined to break up with Eric and let their marriage appeal to the law. Although their marriage ended up divorce, Jennifer treasures her baby as a gift from God. She knows that she should live a better life for her Lisa.

單字片語補充站

01 cheek by jowl
[片] 非常親暱

02 run amuck [片] 發狂

03 call one's bluff [片]
要求對方攤牌、要對方實現其恫嚇

04 bury the hatchet
[片] 言歸和好、休戰

( ) **01.** (A) hang out with   (B) hung out with
        (C) hang up with   (D) hung up with

( ) **02.** (A) have dates   (B) had dates
        (C) had been dated   (D) have dated

( ) **03.** (A) pouring (B) painting (C) showering (D) burning

( ) **04.** (A) have born (B) born (C) was born to (D) gave birth to

( ) **05.** (A) putting over   (B) putting up for
        (C) putting up to   (D) putting up with

( ) **06.** (A) stands (B) stood (C) standed (D) standing

( ) **07.** (A) have spent (B) had spent (C) having spent (D) spent

Who needs grandparents? Children do. And ____1____. Recent studies indicate that ____2____ when they spend large amounts of time together. What is the reason for this? Grandparents give children lots of **affection**[01] **with no strings attached**[02] , and ____3____ at a time when ____4____. Grandparents are a source of **strength**[03] and **wisdom**[04] and ____5____ .

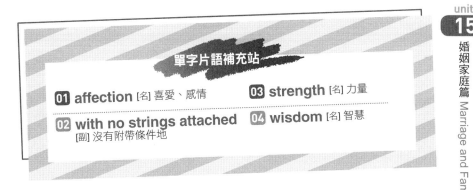

(A) the children make the grandparents feel loved and needed

(B) society may be telling the older people that they are a burden

(C) their grandparents need them

(D) help ease the pressures between children and their parents

(E) grandparents and grandchildren are better off

Unit 15-1: 文章概要及重點理解

　　跨文化關的情侶或夫妻有時候會因許多問題感到不堪負荷。但是，這些夫妻和家庭可以從以下的建議中得到鼓勵。有一些有效的方法，可以解決跨種族婚姻和家庭的問題。

　　對話在所有的關係當中都很重要。來自不同文化的夫妻可能需要投入更多努力來溝通並適應彼此。跨種族的夫妻必須要坦誠以對，互相溝通有關整潔、配偶之間工作的分配、養育小孩的方法、以及教養小孩的原則。

　　在跨文化家庭中，語言、習俗、以及宗教信仰上的差異可能會帶來一些挑戰。但是，這種家庭背景下其實對小孩有一些好處。首先，小孩可以在早期發展階段就自然地學習多種語言。此外，他們可以學習對不同的宗教信仰和行為模式抱持寬容的態度。有了正面的態度，跨文化婚姻可以幫助家庭開啟一段充滿新發現的幸福旅程。

(A) 1. 這篇文章的主題是什麼？
　　　A. 社會學。　　　　　　　B. 地理學。
　　　C. 政治。　　　　　　　　　D. 氣象學。

(A) 2. 下列何者不是文章中所提到跨文化婚姻的潛在問題？
　　　A. 孩子可能會被迫與其中父母親其中一位分開。
　　　B. 夫妻可能會有不同的宗教信仰。
　　　C. 父母親對教養小孩可能會有不同的想法。
　　　D. 語言障礙可能會增加溝通的挑戰性。

(D) 3.根據這篇文章，小孩是可以從跨文化家庭背景中獲得好處的，
　　　只要父母親_____。
　　　A. 尋求社會協助　　　　　　B. 主動參加社區活動
　　　C. 改變他們的習俗和信念　　**D. 可以打開心胸並且抱持寬容態度**

Unit 15-2: 透過克漏字題型強化文法概念

　　五年前，艾瑞克第一次在一場派對上遇到珍妮佛。就在那個時刻，艾瑞克想要在派對結束後約那個有著大眼睛的美女外出逛逛。三

個月之後，在他們經過多次約會後，他們彼此陷入愛河。他們數個月都黏在一起。艾瑞克決定向他深愛的珍妮佛求婚時，當時珍妮佛23歲。他們訂婚，在同一天結婚，當時艾瑞克28歲。因為他們度過了一個很棒、幾乎整晚狂歡的蜜月，珍妮佛懷孕了。

經過十個月之後，珍妮佛產下了一個女嬰名叫麗莎，和母親一樣有著明亮的大眼睛。就在那段懷胎十月期間，珍妮佛幾乎每天都因為懷孕症狀而難搞到不行。起初，艾瑞克很體貼不斷忍受珍妮佛發飆。但是之後，艾瑞克開始和其他外面女生發生性行為來抒發他的情緒。更糟的是，他時常夜宿外面不回家，留下深愛的老婆一個人在家。

後來當艾瑞克在家時，他們開始大吵。這種情形就如同他們已分居一樣。有一天晚上，就在麗莎出生前兩週，珍妮佛再也忍不住放聲大哭，且想找艾瑞克攤牌，她大發脾氣不斷地對艾瑞克大吼，但一點用也沒有。艾瑞克似乎不想重修舊好，僅是面帶微笑地冷眼看著珍妮佛。當時無助的珍妮佛幾乎不再認識站在她面前的男人。所有他們過去共度的快樂時光快速經過她的腦海。她的心已完全粉碎。她唯一在乎的是她要如何和她單親的小孩繼續活下去。於是她轉向求助於艾瑞克，乞求他給這兩個可憐女孩一次機會。但鐵石心腸的艾瑞克只是走開。在珍妮佛渡過了兩週黑暗，寂寞，沒有希望的日子後，珍妮佛決心要和艾瑞克分手。且將他們的婚姻訴諸法律。雖然他們的婚姻以離婚收場，珍妮佛非常珍愛她的女兒，把她視為上天給的禮物。她知道她應該為了小女兒活得更好。

1.A　2.B　3.B　4.D　5.D　6.D　7.B

Unit **15-3: 熟悉篇章的前後銜接關係**

誰需要祖父母呢？小孩子們需要。而(C)他們的祖父母們也需要他們。最近的研究顯示當(E)祖父母和孫子花許多時間在一起，**他們的相處情況便會更好**。其原因究竟如何？祖父母給予小孩許多感情而不附帶條件，在(B)社會上認為年長者是一種負擔之際，(A)小孩子使祖父母有被喜愛和被需要的感覺。祖父母是力量與智慧的來源，並且(D)能幫助減輕子孩子與他們父母之間的壓力。

1.C　2.E　3.A　4.B　5.D

Unit **16-1:** 文章概要及重點理解
閱讀全文，並回答下列的問題

Nothing is more important than good health; therefore, we mustn't take good health for granted. We must keep in mind that the body needs proper care and attention in order to keep healthy. Good health ensures that you have enough energy to do what you want in life. Keeping our bodies in good condition should thus be a priority.

Exercise is the most effective way to achieve this goal. Any doctor will tell us that exercise is an excellent way to prevent sickness and enjoy a better quality of life. Exercising makes us sweat, helps to stimulate blood circulation, and promotes the development of our muscles. Besides, exercise is usually followed by a feeling of relaxation. In addition to keeping us stay healthy, exercise is enjoyable and interesting, especially when done in the company of family or friends. Most important of all, only healthy people have the energy and strength required to chase after lifelong dreams and face everyday's challenges. Thus, proper care should be taken to maintain our mental and physical stability.

( ) 1. Which benefit of exercise is NOT mentioned in the article?

    (A) keep away from illness

    (B) stimulate blood circulation

    (C) lose weight

    (D) create a sense of relaxation

( ) 1. What is the main point of this article?

    (A) to promote a new lifestyle

    (B) to advertise a newly opened gym

    (C) to encourage readers to exercise more

    (D) to teach readers to play a new sport

Propolis[01] is more than just bee **spit**[02]. It is a sort of **sticky**[03] **glue**[04] ____1____ bees use in many ways. They spread it outside their hives ____2____ a poison to keep enemies out. They also use it inside their hives to keep their busy little cities ____3____ .

Propolis is so good at killing **germs**[05] that beehives have cleaner environments ____4____ modern hospitals. Dead **intruders**[06] are even covered with propolis ____5____ their bodies will not rot and bring disease to the **hive**[07].

Long ago, people noticed how bees made use of propolis. They ____6____ propolis' unique **properties**[08] well before modern science figured out what bacteria are. Since propolis kills **bacteria**[09], it is good for stopping____7____ . That's ____8____ ancient Egyptians found propolis useful making **mummies**[10].

單字片語補充站

01 propolis [名] 蜂膠

02 spit [名] 口水、唾液

03 sticky [形] 黏稠的

04 glue [名] 膠水

05 germ [名] 細菌

06 intruder [名] 侵入者

07 hive [名] 蜂窩

08 property [名] 特質、屬性

09 bacteria [名] 細菌的複數

10 mummy [名] 木乃伊

Quiz

( ) **01.** (A) that (B) when (C) in which (D) what

( ) **02.** (A) with (B) in (C) for (D) as

( ) **03.** (A) clean (B) cleaning (C) cleaned (D) to clean

( ) **04.** (A) to (B) with (C) than (D) in

( ) **05.** (A) however (B) so that (C) therefore (D) in order to

( ) **06.** (A) got along with　　(B) took advantage of
　　　　(C) made much of　　(D) got place to

( ) **07.** (A) decrease (B) depress (C) decay (D) dismiss

( ) **08.** (A) why (B) how (C) where (D) which

Many researchers have been interested in whether or not an **individual**[01]'s **birth order**[02] has an effect on intelligence. One of the first studies was carried out in the Netherlands during the early 1970s. ____1____ The test was called the "Raven," which is similar to the I.Q. test. The researchers found a strong relationship between the birth order of the test takers and their scores on the Raven test. ____2____

In 1975, Zajonc and Markus developed the confluence theory to explain the negative effect of birth order on **intelligence**[03] involving the data from the Dutch. ____3____ However, Rutherford and Sewell in 1991 tested the theory and found no **support**[04] for it. They concluded that birth order effects did not exist.

____4____ On one side there are Zajonc and Markus, who state that birth order effects may be explained solely by family size and the **spacing**[05] of births. With short birth **intervals**[06], increasing order of birth will be associated with lower intelligence levels. But with long birth intervals, this pattern may be reversed. ____5____ They show that the **confluence**[07] model does not explain any relationship between birth order and intelligence that may exist in the

American data. Up to date, there is no agreement between these opposing views. And such a **debate**[08] may continue for years to come.

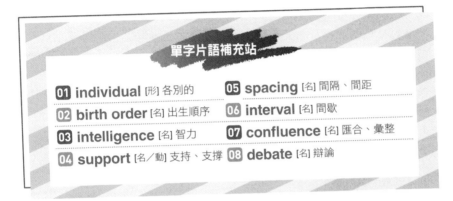

單字片語補充站

01 individual [形] 各別的 　　**05 spacing** [名] 間隔、間距

02 birth order [名] 出生順序 　**06 interval** [名] 間歇

03 intelligence [名] 智力 　　**07 confluence** [名] 匯合、彙整

04 support [名／動] 支持、支撐 **08 debate** [名] 辯論

(A) There are definitely two sides to this issue.

(B) Scores decreased as the family size increased and also with birth order.

(C) An intelligence test was administered to over 350,000 Dutch males when they turned 19 years of age.

(D) On the other side are Rutherford and Sewell, who studied more than 10,000 American high school graduates.

(E) Since then, the theory has been elaborated and even extended to explain the positive effect of birth order on intelligence.

Unit **16-1**: 文章概要及重點理解

健康的身體比什麼都重要,因此我們絕不能把健康視為理所當然。我們必須記得,要保持健康就要妥善照顧及注意身體。有良好的身體狀態,才能確保你有足夠的精力來達成生命中的目標。因此,保持身體健康應是首要之務。

運動是達成此一目標最有效的方法。任何一位醫生都會告訴我們運動是預防病痛及享受優質人生的好方法。運動使我們流汗,有助於刺激血液循環與肌肉發達。此外,運動過後通常會有全身放鬆的感覺。除了可使身體健康,運動讓人感到愉快而且享受其中,特別是和家人朋友一起運動之時。更重要的是,健康的人才具有必須的活力及體力去追逐人生的夢想,以及面對每日挑戰。所以,要維持我們的身心穩定,就必須妥善照顧好身體。

(C) 1. 下列哪一項運動的好處沒有在文章中被提及?
　　　A. 預防疾病
　　　B. 刺激血液循環
　　　C. 瘦身
　　　D. 感到放鬆

(C) 2. 文章的主旨為何?
　　　A. 推廣一種新的生活模式
　　　B. 廣告一間新開張的健身房
　　　C. 鼓勵讀者多運動
　　　D. 教導讀者一項新的運動

Unit **16-2**: 透過克漏字題型強化文法概念

蜂膠不只是蜜蜂的口水,也是種黏膠,對蜜蜂有許多用途。牠們把蜂膠當成毒藥塗在蜂巢外以驅敵人;牠們也把蜂膠用在蜂巢內部,讓牠們忙碌的小小城市保持清潔。

蜂膠的殺菌功效非常卓越,使蜂巢甚至比現代醫院還要乾淨。蜜蜂把蜂膠覆蓋在死亡的入侵者身上,所以這些入侵者的屍體便不會腐爛,也不會把疾病帶進巢。

　　很久以前，人們就注意到蜜蜂如何利用蜂膠。早在現代科學理解什麼是細菌之前，人們就已善用蜂膠的特性。因為蜂膠能殺菌，所以防止腐敗也很有效。這就是為什麼古埃及人用蜂膠使木乃伊防腐的原因。

1.A　2.D　3.A　4.C　5.B　6.B　7.C　8.A

Unit 16-3: 熟悉篇章的前後銜接關係

　　許多研究者對於個人出生順序是否影響其智力一直感到很有興趣。1970年代初期，荷蘭出現了第一個有關此問題的研究實驗。**(C)這項智力測驗的對象是350,000名即將邁入19歲的荷蘭男性**。這個叫做Raven的實驗和智商測驗很相似。研究員發現在參加實驗者的出生順序和他們的測驗成績之間有很大的關聯。**(B)家庭人數多和家中排行較小的參加測驗者測驗成績會較低**。

　　在1975年，Zajonc和Markus根據這項在荷蘭的實驗數據而發展出一套彙整理論，並用此來解釋排行對於智力的負面影響。**(E)從那時起，這項實驗就被用來闡述或延伸解釋家中排行和智力的確切關係**。然而，在1991年，Rutherford和Sewell再度測試這項理論，卻未發現任何可信結果。他們最後總結出：出生順序並不會影響人的智力。

(A)很明確地，對於這個議題存在著兩種不同的觀點。在一方面説來，Zajonc和Markus認為出生順序的影響可以單獨用家庭的人數多寡和小孩出生的間隔時間來解釋。間隔時間一短，越晚出生的孩子就會有較低的智力程度。但間隔時間如果拉長，情況就會相反。**(D)另一方面是Rutherford和Sewell的觀點。他們在美國針對超過10,000名中學畢業生作實驗**。而他們的實驗顯示出這項彙整模式並不能說明在美國相關實驗數據中，出生順序和智力的關係。到目前為止，在這兩項相對的看法之間仍然未達共識。而像這樣的辯論在未來也會持續下去。

1.C　2.B　3.E　4.A　5.D

Killer whales are misunderstood animals. First of all, why killer? Related to the friendly and playful dolphin, killer whales are rarely aggressive. There is no record of a killer whale killing a person in the wild. Why, then, are they called killer whales?

The name comes from sailors who observed some of these whales occasionally hunting other kinds of whales. They were thus given the name, whale killers. Since then, their name has been reversed to become killer whales. In the aspects of their size, the males can grow to be eight meters long and weigh over 5,400 kilograms. Despite their size, they are surprisingly gentle animals. They live together in family groups called pods. They can identify other members of their pod because they share a distinctive accent.

After reading this, do you still think killer whales are dangerous and scary animals?

 **Quiz**

( ) 1. **According to the passage, the name of killer whale were given by_____.**
   (A) some sailors
   (B) a well-known zoologist
   (C) a notorious pirate
   (D) some scholars

( ) 2. **Which of the following statements of killer whale is NOT true?**
   (A) The male ones can grow to be eight meters long.
   (B) They are closely related to dolphins.
   (C) They are solitary animals.
   (D) They have never cause deaths until now.

In 1965, the American statesman, Adlai E. Stevenson, said, "We all travel together, passengers on a little spaceship, ____1____ its **vulnerable**[01] supplies of air and soil. We____2____ to **survive**[02] by the care, work, and love we give our **fragile**[03] **craft**[04]. Our planet is indeed fragile. Every living thing on this planet is part of a complicated ____3____ of life, for no **organism**[05] lives entirely ____4____ . Every organism is affected by all that ____5____ it whether living or nonliving. And ____6____ each organism has some effect ____7____ its surroundings."

Even the most elementary understanding of **ecology**[06] ____8____ knowledge of this cause / effect relationship all organisms have on each other. Everything we do to our environment will ____9____ affect the quality of life we experience on this tiny spaceship. If we want the quality of life to be high, we must be more ____10____ that nature is a finely **balanced**[07] **mechanism**[08] and that it will not **tolerate**[09] the **abuse**[10] we have been giving it.

單字片語補充站

01 **vulnerable** [形] 脆弱的

02 **survive** [動] 活下來、倖存

03 **fragile** [形] 易碎的

04 **craft** [名] 船、飛船

05 **organism** [名] 生物體

06 **ecology** [名] 生態學

07 **balanced** [形] 均衡的

08 **mechanism** [名] 結構

09 **tolerate** [動] 默許、容忍

10 **abuse** [動] 濫用、妄用

 **Quiz**

( ) **01.** (A) dependent on   (B) independent of
         (C) scared of   (D) short of

( ) **02.** (A) manage (B) decide (C) willing   (D) doom

( ) **03.** (A) web   (B) stuff   (C) connection(D) order

( ) **04.** (A) on its own   (B) for its purpose
         (C) together   (D) exclusively

( ) **05.** (A) surrenders (B) surrounds (C) strides (D) submits

( ) **06.** (A) for turn (B) in turn   (C) on turn   (D) by turns

( ) **07.** (A) for   (B) in   (C) on   (D) with

( ) **08.** (A) inquires   (B) requires   (C) acquires   (D) meets

( ) **09.** (A) anyway (B) however (C) in one way or another (D) in way

( ) **10.** (A) understand (B) aware of (C) realize (D) aware

Garbage pollution in Taiwan has become more and more serious recently. ____1____ . They have been dumped at the side of the road and are **giving off**[01] a **disgusting**[02] smell. ____2____ . **Pedestrians**[03] **trample**[04] on the fruit peels, **leftovers**[05] and other **foul**[06] **rubbish**[07]. ____3____ . Garbage pollution is not only destroying the beauty of our island, but also causing great discomfort to us.

In my opinion, building modern **incinerators**[08] and **recycling**[09] plants is a must if we want to solve the problem of garbage. ____4____ -- **reduce**[10] the garbage you create, reuse what you can, and recycle what you can't. It may take a long time to solve the garbage problem in Taiwan, but we have to do it anyway. ____5____ .

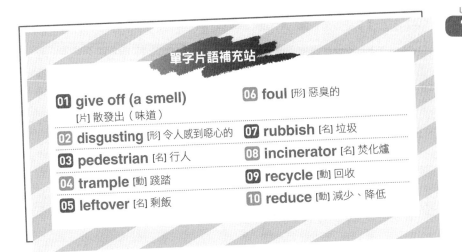

單字片語補充站

01 give off (a smell)
[片] 散發出（味道）

02 disgusting [形] 令人感到噁心的

03 pedestrian [名] 行人

04 trample [動] 踐踏

05 leftover [名] 剩飯

06 foul [形] 惡臭的

07 rubbish [名] 垃圾

08 incinerator [名] 焚化爐

09 recycle [動] 回收

10 reduce [動] 減少、降低

Quiz

(A) In this way, our future generations will be able to live in a clean and beautiful place

(B) Besides, the general public should be familiar with the concept of the "three R's"

(C) Street dogs tear up the plastic bags and scatter the garbage around

(D) Almost every day on my way home, I see piles of garbage

(E) It is a sight that always depresses me

Unit **17-1**: 文章概要及重點理解

殺人鯨是受人誤解的動物。首先,為什麼叫殺人鯨?殺人鯨和友善頑皮的海豚有親屬關係,牠們很少攻擊人。沒有任何記錄顯示殺人鯨曾經在海中殺過人。那麼為什麼牠們會被叫做殺人鯨呢?

這名字來自水手,他們看到有些這種鯨魚偶爾會追別種鯨,因此這種鯨魚就被取名「鯨魚殺手」。從那時起,牠們的名字就被顛倒過來而成為殺人鯨。就他們體型而言,雄鯨可以長到八公尺長,重量超過5,400公斤。儘管體型碩大,他們是驚人溫和的動物。牠們生活在一起,組成叫「群」的家庭。牠們能夠分辨牠們群裡的成員,因為牠們的叫聲有自己獨特的腔調。

讀完本文後,你還認為殺人鯨是危險又可怕的動物嗎?

(A) 1. 根據文章,殺人鯨的名字是來自於＿＿＿＿＿＿?
   (A) 一些水手
   (B) 一個知名的動物學家
   (C) 一個惡名昭彰的海盜
   (D) 一些學者

(C) 2. 下列關於殺人鯨的敘述何者錯誤?
   (A) 雄鯨可以漲到八公尺長。
   (B) 他們和海豚的血緣關係很近。
   (C) 他們是獨居動物。
   (D) 直到現在,他們尚未造成死亡案例。

Unit 17-2: 透過克漏字題型強化文法概念

美國政治家Adlai E. Stevenson在1965年說：「我們是一個小太空船裡旅客，依靠著太空船內微弱的空氣和土壤。我們依賴著自己給予這個脆弱太空船的關心、工作和愛來圖謀生存。我們的行星的確很脆弱。在這一個行星上每一生物是複雜生命網的一部份，因為沒有生物是完全依靠自己而存活的。每一生物被週遭的生物或非生物所影響著，且每一生物交互地對週遭都有某種影響。

即使是對生態有基本的瞭解，也必須瞭解有機體之間的因果關係。我們對環境做的每件事，或多或少都會影響到在這微小的太空船中所體驗的生活環境品質。假如我們要提高生活品質，我們必須意識到大自然是個非常均衡的結構，而且它不會寬容我們對它的濫用。

1.A　2.A　3.A　4.A　5.B　6.D　7.C　8.B　9.C　10.D

Unit 17-3: 熟悉篇章的前後銜接關係

近來，台灣的垃圾污染已經變得越來越嚴重。(D)幾乎每天在我回家的路上，都會看到一堆堆的垃圾。它們被傾倒在路邊，還發出噁心的臭味。(C)流浪狗撕破塑膠袋把垃圾撒了滿地。汙穢的垃圾果皮、剩菜被行人踏來踏去。(E)每次看到這種景象總讓我感覺很糟。垃圾污染不但破壞了這小島的美麗，也令人感到非常不舒服。

依我所見，如果我們想要解決垃圾的問題，建造現代化的焚化爐與資源回收廠是必要之舉。(B)此外，一般民眾也應熟悉「3R」的觀念─減少垃圾產量、重複使用可利用物，以及資源回收。要解決台灣的垃圾問題需要花很久的時間，但是我們仍然必須去解決。(A)如此，我們的後代子孫才能生活在一個乾淨、美麗的家園。

1.D　2.C　3.E　4.B　5.A

Unit 18-1: 文章概要及重點理解
閱讀全文，並回答下列的問題

Entertainment can mean different things to different people; some say being entertained is equal to getting scared. This may mean going to see a scary film or it might mean skiing down steep slopes. Some people, however, seek extreme thrills. They want more danger, and they will do things that most people would never dream of doing, such as an extreme sport called BASE jumping.

There are many dangerous sports, but few of them are considered extreme. BASE jumping fits the label without doubt. It is parachuting, but there is more to it than that. First of all, BASE jumpers are not taken up in airplanes. Instead, they climb to the top of mountains or man-made structures, such as high towers or bridges. The word, BASE, stands for the four types of objects that people can jump from: buildings, antennas (e.g. electric towers), spans (e.g. bridges), and earth (e.g. cliffs). In other words, people jump from something that is very high but is still attached to the ground. Unlike those who jump from airplanes, BASE jumpers do not have much time for their parachutes to open because their jump-off point is always close to the ground.

While this sport is obviously dangerous for everyone, those who jump from buildings probably risk their lives the most. They must be careful of things like power lines, moving traffic, other buildings, and many other <u>obstacles</u>. And when they land, they usually have to watch out for the police as well! Not only is this type of BASE jumping very dangerous, but for obvious reasons, it is also illegal. For some people, though, this only makes this type of extreme sport more exciting.

( ) 1. Which of the following is TRUE?
    (A) Many people stopped BASE jumping for fear of getting arrested.
    (B) BASE jumping from buildings is safer than jumping from towers.
    (C) BASE jumpers jump from buildings and bridges but not airplanes.
    (D) People who BASE jump like seeking thrills as long as they are safe.

( ) 2. The underlined word "obstacles" means .
    (A) things that make progress easier
    (B) things that break the calm
    (C) things that block one's way
    (D) things that interrupt

Unit 18-2: 透過克漏字題型強化文法概念
閱讀全文，並選出空格中該填入的字彙

Humans ____1____ for thousands of years. The first surfers were Polynesian fishermen. They rode their **canoes**[01] out into the ocean in order to catch fish. ____2____ accident, they discovered that they could return to the beach by riding a wooden board. This proved ____3____ the fastest way, and even better, it was fun! Later, Polynesian fishermen began standing up on the wooden boards in the waves. Some of them **settled**[02] in Hawaii and developed the sport even further. It was in Hawaii ____4____ surfing truly became a **recreational**[03] activity. The art of riding the waves would eventually explode ____5____ .

For some serious surfers, surfing has become a way of life. They love challenging nature and chasing freedom. In Hawaii, almost everyone has a surfboard. It has become an important part of their culture. For Americans, during the 1950s, it was a multi-million dollar business. It influenced movies, music, art, and even fashion. For example, Hang Ten was the first clothing company to produce "**baggies**[04]," the long shorts surfers prefer to wear. ____6____ , "baggies" were everywhere. Later, surfing even grew to be ____7____ a symbol of a healthy lifestyle.

Today, surfboards have become more **affordable**[05] and shapers have actually improved the boards themselves by using new technologies. Today's surfboards are lighter and more **durable**[06]. Recently, tow-in surfing has made it possible ____8____ waves of 23 meters, or even higher! Surfers continue to challenge the impossible in their never-ending ____9____ for freedom. With all the changes in the world of surfing, one thing will always remain the same. Surfing is more than just a sport, it is a lifestyle. Surfing ____10____ physical skills, mental focus, and a oneness with the free spirit of the ocean.

單字片語補充站

01 **canoe** [名] 獨木舟   **04** **baggy** [名] 寬鬆短褲、衝浪褲

02 **settle** [動] 定居   **05** **affordable** [形] 可負擔的

03 **recreational** [形] 休閒的   **06** **durable** [形] 耐用的；持久的

 **Quiz**

( ) **01.** (A) have been surfing   (B) has surfed
       (C) are surfing   (D) had been surfing

( ) **02.** (A) With   (B) In   (C) By   (D) After

( ) **03.** (A) in   (B) to be   (C) as   (D) with

( ) **04.** (A) to which   (B) when   (C) why   (D) where

( ) **05.** (A) by no means   (B) in addition
       (C) unluckily   (D) in popularity

( ) **06.** (A) Before long   (B) Long after
       (C) Long ago   (D) Time after time

( ) **07.** (A) referred as (B) regarded as (C) thought of (D) viewed

( ) **08.** (A) that surfing (B) to surf (C) of surfing (D) have surfed

( ) **09.** (A) resemble (B) quest   (C) refine   (D) question

( ) **10.** (A) communicates (B) combines (C) commutes (D) competes

Many people desire to improve their physical **fitness**[01]. ____1____ For people who seek efficient workout **routines**[02] that could be practices at home, Tabata is a good option.

____2____ A Tabata routine includes 20 seconds of intense exercise followed by 10 seconds of rest, and there would be a total of eight rounds. ____3____ Intense exercise like **bodyweight**[03] and **compound movements**[04], such as **burpees**[05], are common to see within those 20 seconds.

Tabata training got its name from Professor Izumi Tabata at National Institute of Fitness and Sports in Tokyo. The research he **conducted**[06] shows that intense workout for only a short time each day may significantly improve the **anaerobic**[07] capacity. ____4____ Then, you can improve both anaerobic and **aerobic**[08] energy supply systems.

Beginners of Tabata training may need to seek advices on the exercise selection to test different muscle groups and avoid **injury**[09]. ____5____ A great variety of other workout type can be found on the online **tutorial**[10] pages or videos of Tabata. You can definitely find the work-out set that suits your physical condition.

單字片語補充站

01 fitness [名] 健身

02 routine [名] 日常運動計畫

03 bodyweight [名] 徒手訓練

04 compound movements [名] 健身組合動作

05 burpees [名] 波比無氧燃脂運動

06 conduct [動] 進行（實驗、研究等）

07 anaerobic [形] 無氧的

08 aerobic [形] 有氧的

09 injury [名] 受傷

10 tutorial [形] 指導的、輔導的

Quiz

(A) Tabata is traditionally a four-minute training technique.

(B) However, the choice of going to the gym may be lost in the crevices between the career, the family activities, and social life.

(C) Some common exercises include thruster, Burpees, and push-ups.

(D) The brevity is its main feature.

(E) That is, you just need to spare s short time pushing yourself as hard as possible at around 90 percent of your maximum heartrate every day.

Unit 18-1: 文章概要及重點理解

娛樂對不同的人來說可以指不同的東西;有的人說被娛樂就等於是受到驚嚇。這可能是指去看個恐怖片或是指從陡坡上滑雪直下。然而有些人追求極端的刺激。他們想要更危險,而且他們會做一般人作夢也不會想到去做的事,像是叫「定點跳傘」的極限運動。

有很多危險的運動,但是很少被當作極限運動。高處跳傘毫無疑問地符合了標準。它是跳傘的一種,但卻不只是跳傘而已。首先,高處跳傘者不是由飛機帶上去的。相反地,他們爬到山頂或人造建物像是高聳的尖塔或是橋墩。BASE的字母代表了人們可以從上跳下的四種物體類型:建築物、天線(比如電塔)、橫跨物(比如橋)和地表(比如懸崖)。換句話說,人們從很高但還是連接著地面的地方往下跳。不同於那些從飛機上跳的人,高處跳傘者沒有太多時間打開降落傘,因為他們的起跳點總是非常靠近地面。

儘管這個運動對每個人來說都是危險的,從建築物上往下跳的人大概是最冒生命危險的。他們必須小心像是電纜、行駛的車流、其他建築物種種東西和許多其他障礙。當他們著陸時,他們通常還得小心警察。原因不但是非常危險,而且很明顯的,它還是違法的。然而對某些人來說,這會讓這種類型的極限運動更為刺激。

(C) 1. 下列何者為真?
  A. 許多人因害怕被抓而停止高處跳傘
  B. 從建築物上跳的高處跳傘比從電塔上跳下更為安全
  C. 高處跳傘者從建築物和橋上跳下但不從飛機上跳
  D. 高處跳傘的人喜歡在安全的條件上追求刺激感

(C) 2. 被畫底線的字指的是?
  A. 讓過程更容易的事物 B. 打破平靜的事物
  C. 擋路的東西 D. 會打擾人的東西

Unit 18-2: 透過克漏字題型強化文法概念

人類衝浪的歷史已達數千年。首次衝浪的是波里尼西亞的漁夫。他們划獨木舟出海捕魚,意外發現可以坐著木板回到海灘。這個方法證明是最快的方法,而且更好的是可以從中取樂。後來波里尼西亞人開始站在浪中的木板上。有些人移居到夏威夷並進一步改善這項運動,衝浪在夏威夷才真正成為一種休閒活動。衝浪的技藝終於廣受歡迎。

對一些認真的衝浪者而言，衝浪已成為一種生活方式。他們喜愛挑戰大自然並追逐自由。在夏威夷，幾乎每個人都有衝浪板。衝浪已經成為夏威夷文化中重要的一部份。在50年代，衝浪在美國是一個百萬元商機的生意，影響了電影、音樂、藝術，甚至時尚。舉例來說，Hang Ten是一家製造「衝浪褲」的服飾公司，這種短褲是衝浪者喜歡穿的七分褲。不久之後，到處都可以見到衝浪褲。後來，衝浪更被視為是健康生活的象徵。

今日，衝浪板的價錢較令人能接受，而製作衝浪板的人的確也以新科技來改善衝浪板。現在的衝浪板更輕更耐用。近年的拖曳衝浪更可讓衝浪者衝上23公尺或更高的浪頭！衝浪者在他們永不止息探索自由中繼續挑戰不可能的任務。衝浪世界的許多變革中只有一件事沒有改變。衝浪不只是一種運動，更是一種生活方式。衝浪結合了身體技能、心智集中以及一種海洋的自由精神。

1.A 2.C 3.B 4.D 5.D 6.A 7.B 8.B 9.B 10.B

Unit 08-3: 熟悉篇章的前後銜接關係

許多人都希望可以身材更健美。**(B) 但是去健身房的機會，常常在追求事業、家庭活動、以及社交生活之間的隙縫溜走了。**對於想在日常生活中養成在家運動習慣的人來說，Tabata會是一個好的選擇。

(A) Tabata傳統上來說，是一種長度為四分鐘的訓練方式。一套Tabata運動包括激烈運動20秒再休息10秒，總共做八個回合。**(D) 耗時較短是它主要的特色。**徒手訓練以及像波比運動等組合健身動作的激烈運動方式，是在這20秒中常做的運動。

Tabata 訓練的名字是來自東京的日本國立體育大學教授Izumi Tabata。他所做的研究顯示每天從事短時間激烈運動可以明顯改善無氧運動能力。**(E) 也就是說，你只需要每天空出一些時間盡量讓自己心跳達到最大值的九成。**那麼，你就可以改善無氧和有氧能量供應的系統。

Tabata訓練的初學者可以尋求建議來選擇適當的運動，測試不同的肌肉群並且避免受傷。**(C) 有些常見的運動包括推進舉重運動、波比運動、以及伏地挺身。**有關Tabata的教學網頁或影片中還可以找到很多不同種類的運動類型。你一定能找到適合自己體能的運動方式。

1.B 2.A 3.D 4.E 5.C

Unit **19-1:** 文章概要及重點理解
閱讀全文，並回答下列的問題

Let's look back in history to the earliest phase of human life. At one time, children didn't have to learn any more than how to cope with their physical environment. They had to learn to be careful moving around objects and to draw back when they get too close to something dangerous. They didn't need a special school to learn these things other than the school of experience. Nor was a school necessary for them to learn how to survive because their parents taught them all they needed to know about how to hunt and to fill the soil. But as societies became more complex, people depended more on others who were living far away. So it became important for children to learn to read and write. When money was created, they needed to learn to count and calculate. Children had to know these things in order to survive in this ever-developing environment. Because such skills could not be learned simply through firsthand experience, schools became necessary so that children could be taught what we now call, the three R's: reading, writing, and arithmetic.

( ) 1. **What did children need to learn in the earliest times?**
    (A) Hunt and farm.
    (B) Draw moving objects.
    (C) Read and write.
    (D) Money counting.

( ) 2. **Why was formal education in schools not necessary for a long time?**
    (A) Parents instructed their children in the "three R's."
    (B) Children taught one another in small supervised groups.
    (C) Children acquired the information they needed by direct experience.
    (D) Teachers came to children's house.

( ) 3. **What change in society first made it important to teach children the three R's?**
    (A) Larger family units and greater financial hardships.
    (B) Outmoded methods of farming and ineffective means of transportation.
    (C) The introduction of a new alphabet and numerical system.
    (D) A new dependence on people far away and the use of money.

In September, many students are entering **university**[01] for the first time. As they leave their childhood friends and **doting**[02] parents, they have **ambivalent**[03] feelings. ____1____ they may feel lonely. In trying to ____2____ new surroundings, they may find the first few weeks somewhat **stressful**[04]. At the same time, ____3____ , they discover that many exciting opportunities await them. Whether it be living in the **residence**[05] halls or participating in **extracurricular**[06] activities, students interact with people of ____4____ interests, tastes and beliefs. Soon new friendships begin to **bud**[07].

____5____ interaction with professors and peers, students evaluate long-held values and **convictions**[08]. They also learn to make decisions ____6____ . Thus, university is a time of freedom and independence.

But students need to learn to make decisions responsibly, ____7____ freedom and responsibility are **inextricably**[09] **intertwined**[10]. They ____8____ their time management skills as they make choices about how to spend their time, where to spend it, and whom to spend it ____9____ . Performing the balancing act between the academic and the social takes intelligent, intentional planning. Undoubtedly, the kind of attitude students embrace and the behaviors they adopt determine the kind of university life they have.

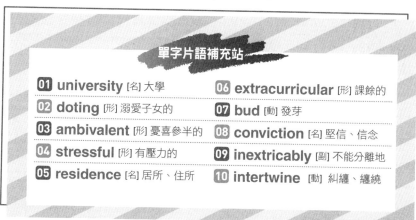

單字片語補充站

01 **university** [名] 大學

02 **doting** [形] 溺愛子女的

03 **ambivalent** [形] 憂喜參半的

04 **stressful** [形] 有壓力的

05 **residence** [名] 居所、住所

06 **extracurricular** [形] 課餘的

07 **bud** [動] 發芽

08 **conviction** [名] 堅信、信念

09 **inextricably** [副] 不能分離地

10 **intertwine** [動] 糾纏、纏繞

 **Quiz**

( ) **01.** (A) Virtually (B) Fortunately (C) Amazingly (D) Initially

( ) **02.** (A) amend by (B) adjust to (C) reply to (D) accustom to

( ) **03.** (A) however (B) therefore (C) despite (D) although

( ) **04.** (A) separating (B) unlike (C) varying (D) disagreed

( ) **05.** (A) At the same time (B) On the basis
(C) In place of (D) As a result of

( ) **06.** (A) on their own (B) all the best
(C) with the crowd (D) in deep water

( ) **07.** (A) whereas (B) except (C) since (D) before

( ) **08.** (A) reject (B) avenge (C) expect (D) sharpen

( ) **09.** (A) to (B) from (C) with (D) for

For those who seek online education resources, Khan Academy and MIT Open course Ware may the already in their favorite website list. ____1____ The online educational platform offers professional courses that build skills in a variety of **specialized**[01] subjects. ____2____ Learners also need to complete **assignments**[02] like weekly exercises and **peer-graded**[03] journals.

____3____ It has offered courses of Master's in **Innovation**[04] and **Entrepreneurship**[05] from HEC Paris. Other certificate programs include Master of Computer Science in Data Science and Master of Business **Administration**[06], both from University of Illinois.

____4____ However, learners can apply for **scholarships**[07] or Financial aids. They just need to **submit**[08] application that specifies their educational background, career goals, and financial **circumstances**[09].____5____ If your application is approved, you can access the degree course on the platform. The scholarships could not be used for the course specified in your **application**[10]. It cannot be transferred across different courses.

單字片語補充站

01 **specialized** [形] 專門的

02 **assignment** [名] 作業

03 **peer-graded** [形] 同儕互相批改的

04 **innovation** [名] 創新

05 **entrepreneurship**
[名] 創業能力、創業精神

06 **administration** [名] 管理

07 **scholarship** [名] 獎學金

08 **submit** [動] 繳交

09 **circumstance** [名] 情況

10 **application** [名] 申請

Quiz

(A) People who are engaged in self-initiated learning through this platform can even get courses of full master's degrees.

(B) The review process may take about two weeks.

(C) Some courses may charge a considerable fee which does not seem to be affordable to everyone.

(D) In recent years, a new choice, Coursera, has been gaining popularity.

(E) There are courses of engineering, humanities, medicine, biology, social science, mathematics, and many other professional fields.

Unit 19-1: 文章概要及重點理解

　　讓我們回顧歷史上人類早期的生活。孩子們曾經只需要學習如何應付自然的環境。他們必須學習在繞著物體移動時要小心，當太接近危險的東西時要後退。他們不需要特別的學校來學習這些事，他們只需要透過經驗來學習。他們也不必從學校學習如何生存，因為雙親教他們狩獵、填土所需知道的一些事。但隨著社會越來越複雜，人們更加依靠早期的其他人。因此，孩子們的學習讀、寫變得重要。當錢幣被創造出來時，他們需學習數數和計算。為了在不斷發展的環境中生存，孩子們必須知道這些事。因為這些技巧無法經由直接的經驗習得，學校教育便成為必要；因此，孩子們被教導我們所謂的3R：讀、寫及算術。

（A）1. 最早時小孩需要學什麼？

　　　A. **捕獵和耕作**　　　　　B. 畫移動的物體

　　　C. 讀寫　　　　　　　　　D. 算錢

（C）2. 為什麼很長一段時間正規學校教育並不被需要？

　　　A. 父母教導它們的小孩3R

　　　B. 小孩們在讀書會中互相監督教導彼此

　　　C. **小孩從直接的經驗中得到所需資訊**

　　　D. 老師會到小孩的家

（D）3. 社會上什麼改變首次使得教小孩3R變得重要？

　　　A. 更大的家庭單位和更大的經濟困難

　　　B. 過時的耕作方法和沒有效率的運輸方式

　　　C. 新的字母表和數字表記系統的引入

　　　D. **對於遠方人們的新的依賴還有錢幣的使用**

Unit 19-2: 透過克漏字題型強化文法概念

　　九月是大學新鮮人入學的季節，當他們離開了兒時的朋友、寵愛他們的雙親，他們有著矛盾的感受。起初，他們可能感到孤獨，為了要適應新環境，剛開始的幾個星期可能會有一點壓力。然而，在此同時，他們會發現有很多刺激的機會在等著他們。學生不管是住在宿舍或者是參加課外活動，不同的興趣、品味、信念讓學生有了互動。很快地，新友誼就要萌芽了。

跟教授或同儕互動的結果，學生評估了長久以來抱持的價值觀和信念，也學習自己做出決定。因此大學是自由和獨立的時期。

但是學生必須要學習如何負責任地做出決定，因為自由跟責任是息息相關的。當學生在決定要如何利用時間、花時間的地點和對象的時候，也同時磨鍊了時間管理的技巧。要在學業跟社交中取得平衡，是需要智慧且刻意的規劃。

無庸置疑的，學生抱持著什麼樣的態度、選擇什麼樣的行為模式，就會決定了他們會過什麼樣的大學生活。

1.D　2.B　3.A　4.C　5.D　6.A　7.C　8.D　9.C

Unit 19-3: 熟悉篇章的前後銜接關係

對尋找線上教育資源的人來說，可汗學院和MIT公開課程可能都已經包含在他們的最愛網站列表之中了。**(D) 近年來有一個新選擇 Coursera越來越受歡迎了。**這個線上教育平台提供專業的課程，可以學習許多不同的專門科目。**(E) 其中包括工程、人文、機械、生物、社會科學、數學、以及其他許多專業領域。**學習者必須要完成每週練習和同儕互評的學習日誌等作業。

(A) 透過這將平臺自發投入的學習者甚至可以修完整的碩士學位課程。它提供巴黎高等商學院的創新與創業碩士學位課程。其他可獲得證書的課程包括伊利諾大學提供的電腦科學與數據科學碩士課程、以及商業管理碩士課程。

(C) 有些課程可能會需要可觀的費用，似乎不是所有的人都負擔得起。但是，學習者可以申請獎學金或補助金。他們只需要繳交申請表，說明自己的教育背景、職涯目標、以及經濟狀況。**(B) 審查約需花兩個星期的時間。**如果申請通過了，你就可以利用這個平台上碩士課程。這個獎學金只能用在你的申請表中註明的課程。無法轉移至其他的課程。

1.D　2.E　3.A　4.C　5.B

Unit 20 **Outer Space**
奧妙宇宙篇

Unit **20-1**: 文章概要及重點理解
閱讀全文，並回答下列的問題

Several tons of material from space rain down on our planet every day, but since most of it comes in the form of minute particles, we seldom take much notice. Things were different in a Chicago suburb on the night of March 26, 2003. That night the skies were lit up by the explosion of a rock estimated to have weighed in the neighborhood of a thousand kilograms and to have been about the size of a refrigerator. Pieces of the object rained down over a wide area, some landing on roads, others smashing through the roofs of homes. Enough fragments were collected so that when combined with eyewitness accounts of the event, it was possible to estimate the space rock's original size, determine its composition, and trace its path through space to Earth.

The object exploded because it hit the atmosphere at 64,000 kilometers per hour. At that speed the difference between the air pressure at the front of the object and that at back could only result in its sudden spectacular destruction.

Whether other such objects vaporize, break apart or reach the surface intact depends on their size, on the angle at which they enter the atmosphere and on what they are made of – fragile stone or more durable iron. Though not an everyday event, explosions like this are probably much more common than the few existing reports of them would indicate. Those occurring over uninhabited areas, including the vast expanses of the oceans would not be seen or heard.

Quiz

( ) 1. According to the passage, what can be said about material that comes to Earth from space?

(A) It is mostly in very small pieces.

(B) It seldom reaches the surface.

(C) It almost never strikes populated areas.

(D) It is not dangerous in any way.

( ) 2. According to the passage, which of the following is true about larger objects entering the atmosphere from space?

(A) They always explode.

(B) They are usually composed of stone.

(C) Some are more likely to survive than others.

(D) They almost never reach ground.

There are two **major**[01] theories ____1____ to explain the creation of the universe. The first is called the "**Big Bang Theory**[02]". It suggests that all the matter in the universe ____2____ once definitely **dense**[03]. An explosion occurred ____3____ matter, energy and even space itself were created. Within a short time matter and energy were **scattered**[04] across the increasing **vastness**[05] of space. The stars, galaxies and planets formed from this original matter. Carried by space expanding ____4____ an moving away from each other at high speed.

The **opposing**[06] theory – the "**Steady State Theory**[07]"– argues that the universe has remained largely the same throughout time. According to this theory the matter that forms the stars, galaxies and the planets, is ____5____ created, to fill the ever-expanding **cosmos**[08] at a constant density. The theory does not attempt to explain how the **matter**[09] ____6____ existence. In proposing a universe in which new matter is continuously created and in which its overall density remains **constant**[10], the steady state view of the creation of the universe is in direct ____7____ with the Big Bang Theory.

單字片語補充站

01 major [形] 主要的

02 Big Bang Theory
[名] 大爆炸理論

03 dense [形] 密集的

04 scatter [動] 散播、撒播

05 vastness [名] 巨大

06 opposing [形] 相對的

07 Steady State Theory
[名] 穩定狀態理論

08 cosmos [名] 宇宙

09 matter [名] 物質

10 constant [形] 不變的

 **Quiz**

( ) **01.** (A) claim (B) that claim (C) claimed (D) to claim

( ) **02.** (A) is (B) were (C) being (D) was

( ) **03.** (A) which (B) for which (C) in that (D) in which

( ) **04.** (A) like (B) alike (C) is like (D) similar

( ) **05.** (A) conservatively   (B) substantially
      (C) continuously   (D) congruently

( ) **06.** (A) comes into (B) arises from (C) goes from (D) gets to

( ) **07.** (A) harmony (B) comparison (C) conflict (D) contact

____1____ What **black holes**[01] are and how they come about are ideas so strange that at first, even astronomers had difficulty accepting them. Now, however, there is no doubt that these strange **bodies**[02] are real. ____2____ Because of this they are truly black. They cannot be seen directly, but scientists can **infer**[03] their **existence**[04] from the effects they have on the orbits of nearby stars and other matter. Black holes are believed to be formed either when a star runs out of **fuel**[05] and **collapses**[06] or when a dying star explodes. ____3____ This powerful **gravitational**[07] force can consume anything close enough to be affected by it. ____4____ Scientists long **suspected**[08] that a black hole existed at a place about ten thousand **light years**[09] from Earth. ____5____

單字片語補充站

01 black hole [名] 黑洞

02 body [名] 物體、東西

03 infer [動] 推斷、推論、猜想

04 existence [名] 存在

05 fuel [名] 燃料

06 collapse [動] 倒塌

07 gravitational [名] 重力

08 suspect [動] 懷疑

09 light year [名] 光年

Quiz

(A) When this happens, energy is emitted by the material just before it is swallowed.

(B) Now, they have detected bursts of X-rays – evidence of matter swirling around a black hole – at just about the same location.

(C) In both cases, matter is compressed with irresistible force and its gravity is concentrated.

(D) Black holes are objects whose gravity is so powerful that nothing – not even light – can escape its grasp.

(E) A black hole is one of the strangest objects in the universe.

Answer 中文翻譯及參考解答

Unit 20-1: 文章概要及重點理解

　　每天都有數以噸計來自太空的物質像下雨般地落到地球上，但是因為其中大多數都是以極微小例子的形式出現，我們很少去注意。但是在2003年三月二十六號夜晚，發生在芝加哥郊區的事情可就不一樣了。夜空被一顆估計約有一個電冰箱大小而重量大約是一千公斤左右的岩石之爆炸所照亮。岩石的碎片灑落在廣大的區域，有些落在道路上，其他則砸穿了房子的屋頂。被收集起來足夠的碎片，再加上目擊者對整個事件的敘述，因而才可能對隕石的大小做出估計，確定其組成的成份，以及追蹤它穿越太空來到地球的路徑。

　　物體之所以會爆炸是因為它以六萬四千公里的時速撞擊大氣層。在如此高的速度之下，物體前後端空氣壓力的差異只能造成它突然而壯觀的破壞。而其他類似的物體是否氣化、裂解還是完整地到達地球表面是與其大小、進入大氣層的角度和構成的物質是脆弱的岩石還是更堅固的鐵質有關。雖然這不是每天都有的事件，但這種爆炸恐怕是比少數有關它們存在的報告所呈現的現象還頻繁。那些發生在沒有人居住的地區，包括廣大的海洋之上的爆炸就不會被看見或是聽到了。

（A）1. 按照短文，下面哪一有關從太空來到地球的物質之敘述是對的？
　　　A. **它通常都是很小的碎片**
　　　B. 它極少抵達地球
　　　C. 它幾乎從來都不會撞擊人口密集的地區
　　　D. 它一點也不危險

（C）2. 按照短文，有關大型物體從太空進入大氣層的敘述何者為真？
　　　A. 它們一定會爆炸
　　　B. 它們通常是由岩石所構成
　　　C. **有些物體較可能比其他物體易存活**
　　　D. 它們幾乎永遠不會抵達地面

Unit **20-2: 透過克漏字題型強化文法概念**

有兩種主要理論試圖解釋宇宙的發生。第一種稱為「大爆炸理論」。它主張構成宇宙的物質起初是極度密集的。在一場爆炸發生之後，所有的物質、能量、甚至於空間都因此而產生。在極短的時間裡，物質和能量擴散到廣闊的空間去。恆星、銀河和行星都是從這些原始的物質而產生。按照此理論，所有的元素至今依然隨著像一個膨脹中的汽泡的空間以極高的速度彼此遠離。

相對的理論——穩定狀態理論——則是認為宇宙恆久以來是維持不變的。按照這種理論的說法，構成恆星、銀河和行星的物質，是不斷地產生出來，填補了持續擴大的宇宙空間，使之維持固定的密度。然而這一理論並沒有嘗試解釋這些新生物的物質到底是如何形成的。當穩定狀態理論提出宇宙不斷生成新物質而且維持固定密度的時候，它與大爆炸理論間的衝突是直接的。

1.B　2.D　3.D　4.A　5.C　6.A　7.C

Unit **20-3: 熟悉篇章的前後銜接關係**

(E)黑洞是宇宙之中最奇特的物體之一。有關黑洞到底是什麼，以及它是如何產生的觀念是如此奇怪，最初就連天文學家都很難接受。到了今日這種奇怪的東西是確定存在了。(D)黑洞的引力如此之強大，**以至於包括光在內的任何東西都逃不出他它的掌握**。就是因為這樣所以它真正是黑的。黑洞無法直接加以觀察，科學家是經由它對周邊恆星以及其他物質的軌道所產生之影響來推論黑洞的存在。

黑洞一般認為是因為恆星的燃料燃燒殆盡之後發生塌陷，或是因為一顆瀕臨死亡的恆星發生爆炸所形成。(C)**這兩種情況都會使物質受到無法抵抗的力量壓縮**，地心引力因而集中。這樣巨大的引力影響所及可以將周邊附近的物質全數消耗。(A)**當此現象發生時，物質在被吞噬之前會釋放出能量**。科學家一直懷疑在距離地球一萬光年處有一個黑洞。(B)**他們如今在差不多相同的位置偵測到大量X射線迸出——這就是物質將被捲入黑洞的證據**。

1.E　2.D　3.C　4.A　5.B

Unit **21-1:** 文章概要及重點理解

閱讀全文，並回答下列的問題

Most of us spend a third of our lives asleep. Scientists have been studying the brain to learn what happens while we sleep. Scientists tell us that there are four stages of sleep. During each stage our brain behaves differently, and so does our body. Each stage is marked by changes in the pattern of brain waves, which can be recorded by machine.

In the first stage, we drift off to sleep. Our muscles begin to relax. Our heartbeat and breathing slow down. Body temperature and blood pressure begin to drop. Stage-two sleep is a time of small, fast brain waves. Our eyes dart quickly from side to side as if watching a movie. This is known as rapid eye movement, or REM sleep. During REM sleep, dreaming takes place. In stage three the brain waves becomes slower again.

Within about 45 minutes after falling asleep, we progress into the fourth stage — deep sleep. As this happens, our brain sends out slower but larger brain waves. This is the most restful kind of sleep, but it is also the time when sleepers are most likely to change positions or sleepwalk. After deep sleep we return to stage two. As the hours pass, we repeat the sleep cycle four or five times. Then we wake up.

Quiz

( ) 1. **What is the main idea of this story?**
    (A) We sleep for many hours.
    (B) Sleep occurs in four stages.
    (C) Deep sleep lasts longest.
    (D) Scientists study sleep.

( ) 2. **At what stage of sleep is a person most likely to change positions?**
    (A) when he first falls asleep
    (B) during stage three
    (C) during REM sleep
    (D) during deep sleep

( ) 3. **When do we dream?**
    (A) during the first stage of sleep
    (B) when brain waves are small and fast
    (C) when brain waves are large and slow
    (D) during the fourth stage of sleep

Sleeping is such a **natural**[01] thing to do. We **spend**[02] **perhaps**[03] ____1____ of our lives doing it. Why, then, do people have trouble sleeping?

Often we can't sleep because something ____2____ is about to happen — a special party or a **championship game**[04], for example. Other times we can't sleep because we are **nervous**[05] or ____3____ .

What can we do if we have **trouble**[06] sleeping? One **suggestion**[07] is to ____4____ a sleep schedule. Whenever **possible**[08], try to get to bed about the same time each night.

____5____ , try to get the right number of hours of sleep for you. Some people may need only six or seven hours of sleep a night. Others may need nine or ten. Seven or eight hours a night is the ____6____ .

單字片語補充站

01 **natural** [形] 自然的

02 **spend** [動] 花費

03 **perhaps** [副] 或許

04 **championship game** [名] 冠軍賽

05 **nervous** [形] 緊張的

06 **trouble** [形] 有問題的、有困難的

07 **suggestion** [名] 建議

08 **possible** [形] 可能的

Quiz

( ) 01. (A) thirty cents (B) one-thirty (C) a third (D) a three

( ) 02. (A) exciting (B) excited (C) excite (D) excitable

( ) 03. (A) relaxed (B) regret (C) sorrow (D) upset

( ) 04. (A) put up (B) set up (C) pick out (D) take over

( ) 05. (A) Instead (B) Also (C) Again (D) Unless

( ) 06. (A) stand (B) regular (C) average (D) common

As exams are around the corner, students try to **make up for**[01] lost time by studying overnight. ____1____ ; however, the reality is much different. Dogs **bark**[02], cicadas **chirp**[03], and family members can be expected to make a **racket**[04] as well, since nobody goes to bed early these days. ____2____.

Last month, as I was trying to review a Mathematics chapter for a test the following day, ____3____ . I shut the door to **block out**[05] the sound, but from my window, I could still hear our neighbors playing **mahjong**[06]. ____4____ . Finally, out of options, I went up on the roof, where I finally found **silence**[07]. ____5____ . I ended up **taking a** short **nap**[08] until deep into the night when everyone else had fallen **asleep**[09], and finished the chapter to the steady sound of my family's **snores**[10].

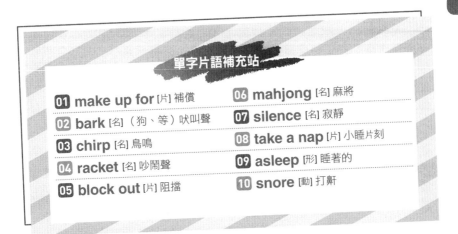

單字片語補充站

01 make up for [片] 補償	**06 mahjong** [名] 麻將
02 bark [名]（狗、等）吠叫聲	**07 silence** [名] 寂靜
03 chirp [名] 鳥鳴	**08 take a nap** [片] 小睡片刻
04 racket [名] 吵鬧聲	**09 asleep** [形] 睡著的
05 block out [片] 阻擋	**10 snore** [動] 打鼾

Quiz

(A) In theory, nighttime should be a perfect time to concentrate, since it is imagined to be both cool and quiet

(B) Unfortunately, I also found a family of mosquitoes, and soon I was returning to my room, itching all over

(C) The evening holds a thousand and one distractions to trouble an unwary student.

(D) I couldn't help overhearing the dialogue from my mother's favorite nighttime soap opera

(E) I decided to study in my sister's room, but she was listening to her radio, and refused to turn it off

Unit 21-1: 文章概要及重點理解

大多數的人把生命的三分之一花在睡眠上。為了瞭解人在睡眠時會發生什麼事，科學家一直在研究人腦。科學家表示，睡眠有四個階段。在每個階段當中，我們的頭腦會有不同的表現，我們的身體亦然。每個階段是以腦波型態的變化為其特徵，而腦波是可以用機器記錄下來的。

在第一階段時，我們不知不覺睡著了。我們的肌肉開始放鬆，心跳與呼吸變得緩慢。體溫與血壓開始下降。睡眠進入第二階段時，腦波短促且急速。我們的雙眼左右急轉，就像在觀賞影片一樣。這段睡眠時間以「眼球急速轉動」著稱，或稱為REM睡眠。在REM睡眠階段，做夢的情形產生。在第三階段當中，腦波再度變得緩慢。

在睡著後45分鐘內，我們進行到第四階段—熟睡。熟睡時，我們的腦子發出較慢 但較大的腦波。這是最平靜的睡眠，但這也是睡眠者很可能改變姿勢或夢遊的時候。熟睡後，我們再回到第二階段。隨著時間過去，我們重覆睡眠循環四到五次，最後我們醒過來。

(B) 1. 這段文章的主旨是什麼？
　　　A. 我們睡很多個小時。
　　　B. 睡眠有四個階段。
　　　C. 深層睡眠持續最久。
　　　D. 科學家研究睡眠。

(D) 2. 人在哪一階段的睡眠中，最可能改變姿勢？
　　　A. 當他剛睡著　　　　　　　B. 在第三階段
　　　C. 在 REM 階段　　　　　　**D. 在熟睡時**

(B) 3. 我們何時會做夢？
　　　A. 第一個睡眠階段　　　　　**B. 當腦波短促迅速時**
　　　C. 當腦波大而緩慢時　　　　D. 第四個睡眠階段

Unit 21-2: 透過克漏字題型強化文法概念

睡眠是一件做起來十分自然的事，我們花了大概有三分之一的生命在睡眠上，但為什麼人們還會有睡眠的苦惱？

我們常常因為某件令人興奮的事即將發生—例如特別的宴會或是一場冠軍賽。其他的時間我們睡不著是因為我們神經緊張或煩亂不安。

如果我們有睡眠上的問題應該怎麼辦呢？建議之一是設定一個睡眠的計劃表。只要可能的話，想辦法每天晚上在相同的時間上床睡覺。

同時，設法找到最適合你自己的睡眠時數。有些人一個晚上也許只要需要六、七個小時，其他人可能需要九到十個小時，平均而言是每個晚上七到八個小時。

1.C 2.A 3.D 4.B 5.B 6.C

Unit 21-3: 熟悉篇章的前後銜接關係

考試即將來臨，學生因此試著藉由熬夜彌補失去的時間。**(A)理論上，夜晚應該是個集中注意力的最佳時機，它被認為是既令人放鬆又安靜的**；不過，事實並非如此。狗吠、蟬鳴、家人也必定會製造很多噪音，畢竟現在這個時代沒有人會早睡。**(C)夜晚包含了許多使人分散注意力的事物以擾亂毫無防備的學生。**

上個月，當我想為了隔天的考試複習一章數學的時候，**(D)我無法阻止自己聽到我母親最喜歡的夜間連續劇的對話。**我把門關上以阻絕聲音，但是還是能透過窗戶聽到鄰居在打麻將。**(E)我決定去妹妹的房間唸書，不過她正在聽廣播，不肯關掉。**終於，我沒有選擇，只好跑去樓頂，那裡果然找到了安寧，**(B)可惜，我也發現了一窩的蚊子；很快我又回到我房間去，全身上下都在癢。**最後我小睡了一下，直到其他人都睡著才起來，然後隨著我家人規律的鼾聲把那一章讀完。

1.A 2.C 3.D 4.E 5.B

Unit 22 **Philosophy**
人生哲理篇

Unit **22-1**: 文章概要及重點理解
閱讀全文，並回答下列的問題

There has never been a family like the Debolts. What makes them so special? The Debolts have conquered problems that would destroy other people. They have not let any obstacles stand in their way.

Robert and Dorothy Debolt have 19 children. Most of their children are adopted, and most are severely handicapped. Several children are crippled; one is blind, and one has no legs. Yet each child has responsibilities to carry out in the house. They work and play together and help each other.

Karen can dress herself, help with the cooking, and even play a musical instrument. These were great achievements for Karen. She was born with no legs and only partial arms. Tich and Anh were injured in Vietnam where they were born. Each uses crutches. Yet they both deliver newspapers every day. J.R. was born paralyzed and soon became blind. The Deblots were told he would never be able to leave his wheelchair. But now he can walk up and down the stairs.

What is the Debolts' secret to success? It is a blend of love and force. They encourage their children to work hard and compel them to do things on their own. They have shown their children that they don't always have to rely on others. Their children believe they can succeed, and so they do.

 Quiz

( ) 1. **According to the author, the reason the Debolts are so special is because _____.**
   (A) all the children in the Debolt family have made great achievements in various fields
   (B) Robert and Dorothy work very hard to bring up 19 children
   (C) Robert and Dorothy are kind to adopt several crippled children
   (D) they have succeeded in overcoming all the difficulties that may ruin other people

( ) 2. **According to this passage, which of the following statements is TRUE?**
   (A) All the children adopted by Robert and Dorothy are native Americans.
   (B) All the children get along well with each other, though most of them are adopted into the family.
   (C) All the children Robert and Dorothy adopt are handicapped.
   (D) To play a musical instrument is an easy task for Karen, a girl with a healthy body.

Helen Keller became blind and deaf when she was one year and seven months old. To communicate, she ____1____ read Braille. She also learned **sign language**[01] and to "hear"-reading lips by touching the mouth of the speaker. The following is an example from her autobiography:

Sometimes I have thought we should live each day as if it ____2____ our last. Most of us, however, take life for granted. The same **casualness**[02] ____3____ the use all our senses. Only the ____4____ appreciate hearing. Only the blind realize the blessings that lie in sight. It's the same old story ____5____ grateful for what we have until we lose it. I have often thought it would be a blessing if each human being were stricken blind and deaf for a few days. Darkness would make him appreciate sight. Silence would teach him the joys of sound.

Now and then I have tested my seeing friends to discover what they see. Recently I was visited by a good friend. She had just returned from a walk in the woods."What did you see?" I asked. "Nothing in particular," was her reply. How is it possible to walk for an hour and see nothing worthy ____6____ ? I cannot see, but I find hundreds of things that interest me. I feel delicate patterns of a leaf. I pass my hand lovingly ____7____ the smooth skin of a birch or the rough **bark**[03] of pine. In spring I touch the branches of trees in search of bud. I feel the velvety texture of a flower. Occasionally, I place my hand on a small tree and feel the happy quiver of a bird in song. At times, I ____8____ to see all these things. If I can get so much pleasure from mere touch, how much more ____9____ must be revealed by sight. Yet those who have eyes see little. The **panorama**[04] of color and action which fills the world is taken for granted.

單字片語補充站

01 **sign language** [片] 手語   **03** **bark** [名] 樹皮
02 **casualness** [名] 漫不經心   **04** **panorama**
　　　　　　　　　　　　　　　　 [名] 全景、一連串景象或事物

( ) **01.** (A) learning　　　　　(B) learned to
　　　　 (C) was learing　　　 (D) has learned

( ) **02.** (A) were (B) was (C) has been (D) had been

( ) **03.** (A) simplifies　　　　 (B) represents
　　　　 (C) characterizes　　 (D) symbolizes

( ) **04.** (A) dumb (B) deafs (C) deaf (D) dumbs

( ) **05.** (A) of being (B) of not being (C) to not be (D) to not being

( ) **06.** (A) notting (B) noting (C) of note (D) of noting

( ) **07.** (A) to (B) by (C) around (D) about

( ) **08.** (A) get (B) long (C) need (D) choose

( ) **09.** (A) beautiful (B) beauty (C) beauties (D) pretty

It is impossible to go through life without any **obstacles**[01].
____1____ However, people of **wisdom**[02] know that "Obstacles
are opportunities in **disguise**[03]." ____2____ Experiences of
learning from obstacles are the most **valuable**[04] **treasures**[05]
of life.

Nowadays we hear **tragic**[06] stories on a daily basic
about people committing **suicide**[07] due to problems in their
financial[08] or romantic lives. ____3____ But, actually, they're
just running away from **reality**[09]. On top of that, they leave
their problems to people who love them or their beloved ones.
____4____ **Nevertheless**[10], life is also full of joy and happiness.
Hence, whenever you're feeling down, definitely seek help.
____5____ .

單字片語補充站

01 obstacle [名] 挫折、障礙　　**06** tragic [形] 悲劇的

02 wisdom [名] 智慧　　**07** commit suicide [片] 自殺

03 disguise [動] 偽裝、掩飾　　**08** financial [形] 財務的

04 valuable [形] 珍貴的　　**09** reality [名] 現實

05 treasure [名] 寶藏　　**10** nevertheless [副] 然而

 Quiz

(A) They may think that ending their own lives is a way to end all their problems.

(B) There's always a way to deal with difficulties

(C) It requires wisdom to transform obstacles into energy.

(D) Many people lost their confidence after they fail to achieve their aim.

(E) Everybody faces frustration and disappointment.

Unit 22-1: 文章概要及重點理解

　　從來沒有一個家庭像戴伯特家一樣。是什麼使他們如此特別？戴伯特家克服了會擊倒別人的困難。他們從不讓做挫折阻撓他們。戴伯特羅伯和太太桃樂西有十九個小孩。他們大部分是認養來的，而且多為嚴重殘疾者。好幾個小孩跛腳，一個眼盲，一個沒有腿。但每一個小孩在家裡都有要履行的責任。他們在一起工作、遊戲、幫忙彼此。

　　凱倫可以自己穿衣服，幫忙煮飯甚至玩樂器。對凱倫來說這是重大的成就。她生下來便沒有腳，只有部分的手臂。提區和安出生在越南時受了傷。他們都用枴杖。但每天他們都去送報紙。J.R.天生癱瘓並在產後不久失去視力。醫生告訴戴伯特夫婦他永遠離不開他的輪椅。但現在他可以上下樓梯了。

　　戴伯特家成功的秘密是什麼？是愛與強迫的融和。他們鼓勵自己的小孩努力工作，強迫他們自己做事。他們向小孩證明了他們不必一直依靠他人。他們的小孩相信他們可以成功，他們也成功了。

(D) 1. 根據作者，戴伯特家如此特別的原因是？
　　　　A. 戴伯特家所有小孩都在各個領域有傑出成就。
　　　　B. 羅伯和桃樂西非常努力養大十九個小孩。
　　　　C. 羅伯和桃樂西很善良地認養了許多殘廢的小孩。
　　　　D. 他們成功地克服了可能會毀了別人的所有困難。

(B) 2. 根據這段文章，下列的敘述何者為真？
　　　　A. 所有被羅伯和桃樂西認養的小孩都是印地安人。
　　　　B. 所有的小孩都相處得很好，儘管他們大多是被認養的。
　　　　C. 所有羅伯和桃樂西認養的小孩都是有殘疾的。
　　　　D. 對凱倫這個擁有健全四肢的女孩來說，演奏樂器並不難。

Unit 22-2: 透過克漏字題型強化文法概念

　　海倫凱勒在一歲七個月時失去了視力和聽力。為了溝通，她學了步萊葉點字法。她也學手語和如何「聽」：靠著碰觸話者的嘴巴讀唇語。以下是她自傳裡的一個實例：

有時候我想我們應該將每一天視為我們的最後一天來過。然後我們大多數人都把生命視為理所當然的。同樣的漫不經心可以用來描述我們對於感官的使用。只有聾子重視聽力。只有盲人瞭解可以看得到是一種賜福。我們不珍惜我們所擁有的直到我們失去為止，這不是新鮮事。我常常想，如果每個人都可以在幾天的期間內遭受盲目和耳聾侵襲，不失為一種祝福。黑暗會令他感激光。寂靜會教導他聲音的喜悅。

我不時會問我看得見的朋友他們看到的東西。最近一個好友拜訪我。她才從林間散步回來。我問：「妳看到什麼？」她回：「沒什麼特別的。」怎麼可能走了一小時沒看到值得提的東西呢？我看不到，但我發現數百件吸引我的事。我感覺到葉片細緻的紋路。我用手深情撫過白樺光滑的表皮和松樹粗糙的樹皮。春日我碰觸樹枝尋找樹芽。我感覺花朵天鵝絨般的質地。偶爾，我將手放在小樹上，感覺到小鳥歌唱的愉悅顫音。有時我渴望見到所有這些事物。如果只透過碰觸我便能得到這麼大的樂趣，透過眼睛該可以看到多美的景象啊。但那些有眼睛的人只看見很少的東西。他們把填滿了色彩、動作的全景世界當作理所當然的一回事。

1.B　2.A　3.C　4.C　5.B　6.C　7.D　8.B　9.B

Unit 22-3: 熟悉篇章的前後銜接關係

人生中不可能沒有挫折。(D)許多人在遭受挫折之後便失去了所有的信心。然而，有智慧的人知道：「挫折是偽裝的祝福。」(C)如何把挫折轉化成動力是需要智慧的。從挫折中學習的經驗是一生之中最珍貴的寶藏。

最近我們每天都會聽到有人因為財務或感情問題而自殺的悲劇。(A)他們可能覺得結束生命就可以解決所有問題，但是他們只不過是逃避現實罷了。此外，他們還把問題留給他們深愛的人和深愛他們的人。(E)每個人都面對挫折和失望。但是換個角度看，生命也充滿了歡欣和喜悅。所以當你感到低潮的時候，一定要尋求協助。(B)事情總會有解決的辦法。

1.D　2.C　3.A　4.E　5.B

Unit 23 Knowledge of Animals
動物知識篇

Unit 23-1: 文章概要及重點理解
閱讀全文，並回答下列的問題

People generally hate cockroaches. They do everything in their power to get rid of them. They put out poisons, set roach traps, and clean every available surface. They even buy electronic devices that are supposed to drive the roaches away. And still the roaches survive.

In fact, cockroaches have been on this earth much longer than human beings. Scientists consider them to be one of the earliest forms of life still in existence. What accounts for their ability to survive? Well, for one thing, they seem to be able to live any place, hot or cold, damp or wet. For another thing, they don't need much food. They can go without eating for several weeks. Also, they can eat almost anything: wallpaper, glue, books, dirty laundry. It doesn't make much difference what — it's all part of the roach diet.

Cockroaches seem very adaptable. Regardless of what kind of poison is set out for them, they seem to adjust very quickly to it. If they are somehow eliminated from one part of the house, they simply move to a different part. The war of human against roaches is likely to continue for a long time to come.

Quiz

( ) 1. **According to the passage, which of the following is NOT mentioned as a reason for the survival of roaches?**
(A) They adjust quickly to poisons.
(B) They can eat anything.
(C) They can reproduce.
(D) They can live any place.

( ) 2. **All of the following are mentioned as a way to get rid of roaches EXCEPT for _____.**
(A) roach traps
(B) loud noises
(C) keeping things clean
(D) poisons

( ) 3. **Why will war against roaches continue for a long time?**
(A) Because people don't mind roaches very much.
(B) New ways will be found to fight against roaches.
(C) Because people enjoy fighting against roaches.
(D) Because the roaches will find a way to survive.

Well goes an old saying, "Dogs are the best friends of human beings." There is no ____1____ that dogs play a very **significant**[01] role in human daily life. They are ____2____ **obedience**[02], loyalty. For some people, the companionship a dog provides is ____3____ that from friends or family, ____4____ that he can be a **deterrent**[03] against thieves. Yet, with more and more people deserting them and the consequent multiplication, a large number of stray dogs are wandering in the streets, or even on campus, posing a risk not only to the surroundings but also to our health.

Such is the case. It is high time that we should take some measures to solve the problem. The following are my suggestions. First of all, the government should draw up a plan about how to catch stray dogs and deal with them. In the second place, the school should **enhance**[04] education. They should teach their children the right **concept**[05] of raising pet dogs, for education is the best way to **solve**[06] problems. ____5____, we should think twice before keeping a dog. Make sure that we will take care of it no matter what happens. Keeping a dog **indeed**[07] brings some people **pleasure**[08], but in the case of stray dogs, we also have to be **realistic**[09] and face the problems they create. ____6____ we take the problem of stray dogs seriously can the problem be solved.

單字片語補充站

01 **significant** [形] 重要的

02 **obedience** [名] 服從、馴服

03 **deterrent** [名] 制止物、威懾力量

04 **enhance** [動] 增加、加強

05 **concept** [名] 概念

06 **solve** [動] 解決

07 **indeed** [副] 確實

08 **pleasure** [名] 樂趣

09 **realistic** [形] 實際的

 Quiz

( ) **01.** (A) denying (B) doubted (C) deny (D) undoubtedly

( ) **02.** (A) famous by (B) known for (C) known of (D) famous of

( ) **03.** (A) most valued (B) more value
(C) more valuable than (D) valuable more

( ) **04.** (A) not to mention (B) without mention
(C) just to mention (D) needless mention

( ) **05.** (A) What's worse (B) Most important of all
(C) After all (D) Indeed

( ) **06.** (A) Until (B) Before (C) Only when (D) Otherwise

There are more than 50 different kinds of **kangaroos**[01] in the world today. ____1____ . Kangaroos cannot walk or run. They just jump. ____2____ because they spend the daytime **snoozing**[02] in the shade.

Straight[03] after they are born, the joeys (baby kangaroos), which are only about two-and-a-half **centimeters**[04] long, have to **drag**[05] themselves to their mother's **pouch**[06]. ____3____ . They stay in the pouch until they are eight months old. After that, they leave home for good . ____4____ . A 50 pound joey, ____5____ , was once found still living in its mother's pouch.

Have you ever **wondered**[07] why these animals are called "kangaroos"? Well, ____6____ , when Captain Cook landed in Australia and heard the **aborigines**[08] calling these amazing animals "Kangooroo, "he wrote the name down as "kangaroo." That's how this animal got its name.

單字片語補充站

01 kangaroo [名] 袋鼠

02 snooze [動] 打盹

03 straight [副] 直接地

04 centimeter [名] 公分

05 drag [動] 拉、拖著

06 pouch [名] 育兒袋

07 wonder [動] 想知道

08 aborigine [名] 原住民、土著

Quiz

(A) The best time to see kangaroos in action is the evening and early morning

(B) for example

(C) The smallest ones are only five centimeters tall but the biggest are more than two meters

(D) according to one story

(E) Sometimes the joeys aren't too keen on making their way in the big wide world

(F) they find their way there by following the pattern of their mother's hairs

Unit 23-1: 文章概要及重點理解

人們大都討厭蟑螂。他們極盡所能想除掉蟑螂；他們會放毒藥、設下補蟑螂的陷阱，清理每個蟑螂出沒的地方。他們甚至會買些設計來驅除蟑螂的電子裝置。可是蟑螂依然活了下來。

事實上，蟑螂生活在地球上遠比人類來得久遠。科學家認為蟑螂是現存最早的生命形式之一。是什麼使得蟑螂能夠活下來呢？嗯，一來，牠們能在任何地方生存，不管是冷或熱、乾或濕。另一方面，牠們不需太多的食物。牠們可以好幾個禮拜都不吃東西。此外，牠們什麼都吃：壁紙、膠水、書、髒衣服，什麼東西都無所謂，全都是蟑螂食物的一部份。

蟑螂似乎適應力很強。不管人們放哪一種毒藥，牠們似乎很快就能適應。要是牠們莫名其妙地消失在房子的某部份，那麼一定是搬到另一個地方去了。人和蟑螂之間的戰爭很可能在未來還得繼續下去。

(C) 1. 根據本文，下列哪一項不是蟑螂活下來的原因？
　　　A. 牠們很快就能適應毒藥。　　B. 牠們什麼都能吃。
　　　C. 牠們能迅速繁殖。　　　　D. 牠們能生活在任何地方。

(B) 2. 下列所提到的都是驅除蟑螂的方法，除了 ＿＿＿＿＿＿ 以外。
　　　A. 蟑螂陷阱　　　　　　　　　**B. 巨大的聲響**
　　　C. 保持東西的清潔　　　　　　D. 下毒

(D) 3. 為什麼和蟑螂的戰爭將會持續很長的一段時間？
　　　A. 因為人們不介意蟑螂。
　　　B. 將有新方法去對抗蟑螂。
　　　C. 因為人們喜歡和蟑螂作對。
　　　D. 因為蟑螂總有辦法活下去。

Unit 23-2: 透過克漏字題型強化文法概念

俗話說的好，狗是人類最忠實的朋友。無庸置疑地，狗在人類日常生活中扮演了非常重要的角色。牠們以服從、忠實著稱。對某些人而言，狗的陪伴提供了比朋友或者家人的陪伴更多的價值，更不用說牠可以遏止小偷。然而，越來越多人把牠們遺棄，隨之而來繁衍的量讓大量的流浪狗在街上甚至在校園內閒晃，造成不止對環境還有對我們的健康威脅。

　　情況即是如此。該是我們採取一些措施來解決這樣的問題的時候了。以下是我的建議。首先，政府應該要擬定計畫有關於如何捕捉流浪狗及安置牠們。再者，學校方面應該要強化教育。應該要教導小孩子正確的飼養寵物狗的觀念，因為教育是最好的解決方式。最重要的是，我們每一個人應該在飼養寵物狗前三思。我們應該要確認無論牠發生什麼事，我們都會好好照顧牠。養小狗確實可以帶給一些人快樂，但是就流浪狗而言，我們也必須要很務實，而且必須要面對牠們所製造的問題。只有我們認真地處理流浪狗的問題，這個問題才會得到解決。

1.A　2.B　3.C　4.A　5.B　6.C

Unit 23-3: **熟悉篇章的前後銜接關係**

　　今天世界上有多於五十個不同品種的袋鼠。**(C)最小的一種，身高僅有五公分，但是最大卻超過兩公尺高。**袋鼠不能行走或是奔跑。他們只能用跳的。**(A)觀賞袋鼠活動的最佳時機在夜晚或者是早晨，**因為他們白天都在陰影處打瞌睡。

　　當小袋鼠們一出生，袋鼠的幼獸（也就是袋鼠寶寶）只有二點五公分長，他們必須吸附在母親的育兒袋上面。**(F)牠隨著母親毛髮的毛流花色找到育兒袋的位置。**他們會待在育兒袋裡直到他們八個月大。在那之後，牠們就會永遠離開家裡。**(E)有時候小袋鼠不會積極想要探索外面的廣大世界。(B)舉例來說，**曾經有一隻50磅的小袋鼠被發現還住在媽媽的育兒袋內。

　　你是否曾經納悶為什麼這些動物要叫做「Kangaroo」呢？嗯，**(D)根據一個故事的說法，**當Cook船長在澳洲登陸時，他聽到原住民叫這些神奇的動物為「Kangaroo」，他就寫下牠們的名字為「Kangaroo」。這就是這個動物名字的由來。

1.C　2.A　3.F　4.E　5.B　6.D

Unit 24 Language Origin
追溯語言篇

Unit 24-1: 文章概要及重點理解
閱讀全文，並回答下列的問題

Human language is a living thing. Each language has its own biological system, which makes it different from all other languages. This system must constantly adjust to a new environment and new situations to survive and flourish.

When we think of human language this way, it is an easy step to see the words of a language as being like the cells of a living organism - they are constantly forming and dying and splitting into parts as time changes and the language adapts.

There are several specific processes by which new words are formed. Some words come into the language which sounds like what they refer to. Words like buzz and ding-dong are good examples of this process.

Still another way in which new words are formed is to use the name of a person or a place closely associated with that word's meaning. The words sandwich and hamburger are examples of this word - formation process. The Earl of Sandwich, an English aristocrat, was so fond of gambling at cards that he hated to be interrupted by the necessity of eating. He thus invented a new way of eating while he continued his game at the gambling table. This quick and convenient dish is what we now call a sandwich - a piece of meat between two slices of bread. After that, hamburgers became the best-known kind of sandwich in the world after it was invented by a citizen of Hamburg in Germany. As long as a language is alive, its cells will continue to change, forming new words and getting rid of the ones that no longer have any use.

( ) 1. The passage is mainly about

(A) the biological system of a living organism.

(B) the inventors of sandwich and hamburger.

(C) the development of human cells.

(D) the changes of a language.

( ) 2. A language is a living thing in many ways EXCEPT

(A) It is similar to the biological system of a living organism.

(B) It actually has many living cells that split and form constantly.

(C) It must adjust to new environments to survive.

(D) Its old words die out while new words are constantly added.

( ) 3. The word sandwich came from

(A) card games. (B) a piece of meat.

(C) a person's name. (D) a place in England.

Idioms[01] and **proverbs**[02] add color to a language, and they also **reveal**[03] some of the culture behind the language. ____1____ the most interesting example is the expression, "rain cats and dogs."Does it mean that cats and dogs ____2____ come down from the sky? Some people in 17th-century England did believe ____3____ , since many dead bodies of cats and dogs were found ____4____ around after a heavy fall of rain. ____5____ , this idiom simply means "rain very hard." There are two more **explanations**[04] as to ____6____ this idiom **came into being**[05]. One comes from the Greek word catadupa, ____7____ "**waterfall**[06]." People ____8____ often thought of waterfalls when it rained heavily. Since catadupa sounds like "cats and dogs," heavy rains came to be described ____9____ falling cats and dogs. ____10____ **stems from**[07] the belief of ancient weather **prophets**[08] that rain was caused by the evil **spirits**[09] of cats and dogs.

單字片語補充站

01 idiom [名] 習語、成語　　**06 waterfall** [名] 瀑布

02 proverb [名] 諺語　　**07 stem from** [片] 起源於

03 reveal [動] 展露、顯露出　　**08 prophet** [名] 先知、預知者

04 explanation [名] 解釋　　**09 spirit** [名] 靈、精神

05 come into being
[片] 形成、生成

 **Quiz**

( ) **01.** (A) Possibly　(B) Basically　(C) Generally　(D) Accidentally

( ) **02.** (A) fairly　(B) safely　(C) actually　(D) hardly

( ) **03.** (A) it　(B) these　(C) those　(D) them

( ) **04.** (A) fooling　(B) swimming　(C) wandering　(D) floating

( ) **05.** (A) As a result　(B) In fact　(C) At last　(D) In addition

( ) **06.** (A) what　(B) when　(C) how　(D) where

( ) **07.** (A) means　(B) meant　(C) meaning　(D) it means

( ) **08.** (A) the other day　　(B) in those days
(C) for days　　(D) these days

( ) **09.** (A) of　　(B) to　　(C) in　　(D) as

( ) **10.** (A) The other　(B) The last　(C) The another　(D) The next

You might hear people speak of languages as living or as dead. While we cannot think of language as plants or animals that **possess**[01] life apart from the people who speak it, we can **observe**[02] in speech the process of change that **characterizes**[03] the life of living things. ____1____, we call it a dead language. Take Classical Latin as an example. ____2____. **Therefore**[04], it is a dead language.

On the other hand, English, like other languages, is in **constant**[05] growth and **decay**[06]. Vocabulary of a language is the best example to **demonstrate**[07] the process of constant change. For example, ____3____. Even existing words may change in meaning. ____4____. Thus, the language used one thousand years ago can be **unintelligible**[08] to those who are using its modern form.

單字片語補充站

01 possess [動] 擁有

02 observe [動] 觀察

03 characterize [動] 以……為特徵

04 therefore [副] 因此

05 constant [形] 長期的、連續發生的

06 decay [動] 腐蝕、衰弱

07 demonstrate [動] 表明

08 unintelligible [形] 無法理解的

 Quiz

(A) It has not changed for almost two thousand years

(B) Changes can also occur in the pronunciation and the grammatical forms of a language

(C) When a language stops to change

(D) much of the vocabulary of Old English has been lost, while new words have been developed and added

Unit 24-1: 文章概要及重點理解

人類的語言是活的東西。每一個語言都有使它自己和別的語言區隔的生物系統。這個系統必然要不停地調整自己來適應新的環境和情況以便存活和成長茁壯。

當我們用這種方式看待語言時，我們便可以不費工夫地將語言的世界視為生物有機體的細胞——他們持續地形成和死去，隨著時間和語言的適應而分裂。

新字被形成有幾個特別的過程。有些字進入語言中，它們聽起來就像它們所表達的意思一樣。像是buzz（嗡嗡）和ding-dong（叮咚）就是這個過程的好例子。

還有另一種新字形成的方法是使用一個強烈和字的意義結合的人名或地名。這種造字過程的例子是字詞像是sandwich和hamburger。山德文治伯爵喜歡紙牌賭博，他討厭因為要吃東西而被迫停下來。因此他發明了一種新的吃法讓他可以繼續在賭桌上玩遊戲。這道快速而方便的料理就是現在我們說的三明治——在兩片麵包中夾著一片肉。接著，在被一位漢堡的居民發明之後，漢堡成為了世界上最廣為人知的一種三明治。

只要語言是活的，它的細胞就會持續改變，產生新字並且拋棄不再使用的字。

(D) 1. 這篇文章主要是關於？
    A. 有機體的生物組織
    B. 三明治和漢堡的發明者
    C. 人類細胞的發展
    D. 語言的改變

(B) 2. 語言在很多方面是活的除了？
    A. 它和有機體生物組織十分類似
    B. 它真的有許多活的細胞會不停分離和自組
    C. 它必須適應新的環境來生存
    D. 當新字不斷增加時舊字會滅絕

(C) 3. 「三明治」這個字來自於？

    A. 卡片遊戲   B. 一片肉

    C. 一個人的名字   D. 英國的一個地方

Unit **24-2: 透過克漏字題型強化文法概念**

　　俗語和諺語為一個語言增添了色彩，他們也透露出了一些語言背後的文化。最有趣的例子可能是「雨落下狗與貓」的說法。這真的意味著狗和貓自天空落下嗎？十七世紀有些英國人的確如此相信著，因為在一場大雨後河邊可以發現許多死去貓狗的屍體漂浮。事實上，這個習語不過就是「雨下得很大」的意思。關於這個習語如何產生還有兩個解釋。一個是來自希臘文字catadupa，意思是瀑布。那時候雨下很大時人們常想到瀑布。因為catadupa聽起來像 cats and dogs，雨落下貓和狗便被用來形容大雨了。另一個說法起源於自古代天氣預言者相信雨是貓和狗的惡靈所造成的。

1.A 2.C 3.A 4.D 5.B 6.C 7.C 8.B 9.D 10.A

Unit **24-3: 熟悉篇章的前後銜接關係**

　　你可能聽人說過語言是活的或是死的。雖然我們不能想像語言像植物或動物一樣，擁有像說他們的人一樣分別的生命，我們仍可以在言談中觀察到有生物生命特徵的改變過程。**(C)當一個語言停止改變時**，我們稱呼它為死的語言。拿古典拉丁語作例子。**(A)它幾乎兩千年來都沒有改變**。因此，它是死的語言。

　　另一方面，英語就像其他語言，持續成長與衰弱。一個語言的詞彙是證明其持續改變的最好例證。舉例而言，**(D)許多古英語的詞彙已經遺失，然而新字卻在發展和增加當中**。即使現存的字也會改變意義。**(B)改變也會發生在語言的發音和文法形式上**。因此，一千年前使用的語言可能是對使用它現代形式的人無法理解的。

1.C 2.A 3.D 4.B

Unit 25-1: 文章概要及重點理解
閱讀全文，並回答下列的問題

On an island in New York harbor stands a lady holding a torch high over her head. She is not a real living lady, but a statue. She is called the Statue of Liberty.

There are small boats used only to take visitors to and from the island. People climb a winding stair inside the Statue of Liberty and look out over the harbor from the crown on her head. Forty persons can stand in her head at one time. She is about fifteen times as high as the wall of your schoolroom. This statue was a gift to the United States from the people of France to celebrate her one hundredth birthday as a nation in 1886.

( ) 1. **The Statue of Liberty is** _____.

    (A) more than one hundred years old now

    (B) less than one hundred years old now

    (C) exactly one hundred years old now

    (D) as old as the United States

( ) 2. **Most visitors reach the statue** _____.

    (A) by train

    (B) by climbing

    (C) by boat

    (D) by swimming

( ) 3. **The Statue of Liberty was** _____.

    (A) given to France

    (B) bought by the United States

    (C) bought by New York

    (D) given by the people of France

( ) 4. **People climb to the top of the statue** _____.

    (A) because the stairs wind

    (B) to look over the harbor

    (C) to see how big it is

    (D) to stand in the head

A young couple that had **received**[01] many **valuable**[02] **wedding**[03] presents ____1____ their home **in a suburb**[04].

One morning, they ____2____ in the mail two tickets ____3____ a popular show in the city, with a single line.

"Guess who **sent**[05] them."

The couple had ____4____ **amusement**[06] in trying to find out who the kind person was, but ____5____ in the **effort**[07]. They attended the theater, and had a **pleasant**[08] time. ____6____ their return home late at night, still ____7____ to guess who in the world had sent them the tickets, they found the house____8____ everything valuable. On the table in the kitchen ____9____ a piece of paper____10____ was written **in the same hand**[09] as the note with the tickets. "Now you know."

單字片語補充站

01 **receive** [動] 接收到

02 **valuable** [形] 有價值的

03 **wedding** [名] 婚禮

04 **in a suburb** [片] 在郊區

05 **send** [動] 郵寄

06 **amusement** [名] 樂趣、趣味

07 **effort** [名] 努力

08 **pleasant** [形] 令人愉快的

09 **in the same hand**
[片] 相同字跡

( ) **01.** (A) passed by (B) picked up (C) carried away (D) established

( ) **02.** (A) accepted (B) found (C) reached (D) receipted

( ) **03.** (A) in (B) at (C) for (D) on

( ) **04.** (A) much (B) many (C) very (D) more

( ) **05.** (A) failing (B) to fail (C) fail (D) failed

( ) **06.** (A) When (B) While (C) In (D) On

( ) **07.** (A) tried (B) trying (C) to try (D) try

( ) **08.** (A) stripped (B) stripping (C) stripped of (D) stripping of

( ) **09.** (A) had (B) was (C) were (D) having

( ) **10.** (A) on which (B) in that (C) which (D) that

Giving gifts at a business **occasion**[01] is not common in British culture. ____1____ However, it could be appropriate to give a thought item as a **commemorative**[02] **gesture**[03] for the occasion to mark the conclusion of a deal. ____2____ Consider whether the gift can be something that the **recipient**[04] would gladly display in the living room rather than consign it in the attic. Here are some suggestions to choose a tasteful and not **ostentatiously**[05] expensive gift.

____3____ A porcelain with a unique **inscription**[06] can also be a pleasant thing to offer. You can also bring small gifts like a pen or a book suitably inscribed to the meeting. Sending a card to the business **associate**[07] to express **gratitude**[08] is also a good way to maintain valuable contacts. ____4____

You might also have chances to visit the British colleague at his place. Then, bringing wine, flowers, or chocolate for the host would be the standard practice. A fine vintage claret may be appreciated. ____5____ When choosing flowers, keep the European **caveats**[09] in mind: no red roses, white lilies, or **chrysanthemums**[10]. Finally, it would be thoughtful to send a hand-written note to the host for any hospitality.

單字片語補充站

01 occasion [名] 場合

02 commemorative
[形] 紀念性的

03 gesture
[名] 示意動作、象徵性的行動

04 recipient [名] 接收者

05 ostentatiously
[副] 誇張地

06 inscription [名] 題詞、題字

07 associate [名] 合作夥伴

08 gratitude [名] 感激

09 caveat [名] 警告、告誡、限制條款

10 chrysanthemum [名] 菊花

Quiz

(A) Make sure that it's a carefully chosen gift.

(B) Your British colleague might feel embarrassed to receive any gift at a business meeting.

(C) Some delicate items made of gold or silver may be good choice.

(D) Campaign can be welcome for an after-dinner toast.

(E) Another possible way is offering a meal or buying a round of drinks for the British colleagues after work.

Unit 25-1: 文章概要及重點理解

在紐約港一個小島上，佇立一位將火炬高舉過頭的女士。她不是一個真正活生生的女士，而是一座雕像。她被稱為自由女神像。

有許多小船只用來載送遊客往返這個小島。人們爬上自由女神像內一道蜿蜒階梯，從她頭上的皇冠俯瞰整個港口。她的頭部內可同時站立四十人。她大約是你教室牆壁的十五倍高。

這座雕像是法國人民在一八八六年送給美國，慶祝美國建國一百週年的禮物。

(A) 1. 自由女神像＿＿＿＿＿。
　　　 A. **超過一百年了**
　　　 B. 不超過一百年
　　　 C. 現在正好一百年
　　　 D. 跟美國一樣老

(C) 2. 大多數的旅客如何到達自由女神像？
　　　 A. 搭火車
　　　 B. 攀爬
　　　 C. **搭船**
　　　 D. 游泳

(D) 3. 自由女神像＿＿＿＿＿。
　　　 A. 給了法國
　　　 B. 是由美國買下的
　　　 C. 是被紐約市買下的
　　　 D. **是由法國人民贈送的**

(B) 4. 人們爬到雕像頂端＿＿＿＿＿。
　　　 A. 因為雕像很蜿蜒
　　　 B. **眺望港口**
　　　 C. 看它有多大
　　　 D. 為了站在它頭上

Unit 25-2: 透過克漏字題型強化文法概念

　　一對收到了許多結婚禮物的年輕夫婦，在郊區成立了家庭。一天上午他們收到兩張在城裡演出的通俗劇入場券，並附有簡單的一行字：

「猜猜誰送的票？」

　　這對夫婦好奇地想找出那個好心人，但沒能成功。他們去看了戲，並享受美好的時刻。當他們深夜回到家裡時，仍在猜到底誰送他們戲票，但他們發現家裡值錢的東西已被洗劫一空。在廚房的桌子上有一張紙條，上面用與送票來的紙條上一樣的字體寫道：

「現在你知道了。」

1.D　2.B　3.C　4.A　5.D　6.D　7.B　8.C　9.B　10.A

Unit 25-3: 熟悉篇章的前後銜接關係

　　商業場合送禮物在英國文化中並不常見。**(B) 你的英國同事在商業會面時收到禮物的話，可能會覺得尷尬。**但是，如果是在慶祝案子完成的場合，送個精心挑選的禮物作為紀念可能是很適當的。**(A) 一定要送個細心挑選的禮物。**思考一下，收到的人會很高興地把這個禮物放在客廳陳列，還是會把它束諸高閣。以下有些建議，是可以選到有品味但又不會貴得很誇張的禮物。

　　(C) 有些金或銀的精緻物品會是不錯的選擇。有獨特題字的瓷器會是個受歡迎的禮物。你也可以帶一些有題字的筆、或者是書等等的小禮物來開會。寄卡片給商業夥伴來表達感謝也是維持聯繫的好方法。**(E) 另一個可能的方式是在工作結束後請你的英國同事吃飯或喝飲料。**

　　你可能也會有機會去拜訪英國同事的家。那樣的話，通常都會帶酒、花、或者巧克力。陳年紅葡萄酒是很不錯的選擇。**(D) 香檳則是適合餐後敬酒用。**在歐洲，選擇要送人的花，要記得避免紅玫瑰、白色百合、或菊花。最後，用手寫卡片感謝主人款待也是很貼心的舉動。

1.B　2.A　3.C　4.E　5.D

Unit 26-1: 文章概要及重點理解
閱讀全文，並回答下列的問題

There are five members in my family. I am the eldest child and I have two brothers. My father is a government official, who is very devoted to his work. My mother is a housewife and a good chef. She appreciates Chinese calligraphy very much. One of my brothers is three years younger than me, but he surpasses me in knowledge and wisdom. My other brother is only twelve years old. As for me, my hobbies are stamp collecting and listening to classical music.

On weekends, my family usually get together to engage in some activities, such as having a picnic or a party. However, this weekend will be very special as we are to entertain four relatives, including my uncle, aunt and two cousins. Father cleaned the windows and painted the roof green. Mother did the dishes and made the beds. My brother watered the flowers and I swept the floor. All of us were very tired but we were very happy. My cousins will play on-line games with me and I hope they can come soon.

( ) 1. **Which one below is the writer's hobby?**

   (A) listening to music

   (B) making stamps

   (C) reading classic literature

   (D) watching TV program

( ) 2. **What does the family usually do on weekends?**

   (A) staying at home

   (B) going to movies

   (C) having a party

   (D) visiting the writer's grandparents

I had been sitting by myself in my usual compartment for at least ten minutes, waiting ____1____ . The trains from Littlebury never seemed to start ____2____ and I often thought that I could have **lain**[01] in bed a little longer or had another cup of tea before leaving home. Suddenly I heard someone shouting on the **platform**[02] outside. A young girl was running towards the train. The man ____3____ put out his hand to stop her, but she ran past him and opened the door of my **compartment**[03]. Then the **whistle**[04] blew and the train started.

"I nearly missed it, ____4____ ?" the girl said. "How long does it take to get to London?"

"It depends on the ____5____ ." I said. "Some days it's ____6____ others."

"I'll have to have my watch so as not to be late again tomorrow," she said. "It's my first day at work in a new firm today and they told me that the man ____7____ is very **strict**[05]. I haven't met him yet, so I don't know what he is like, but he sounds a bit frightening."

She talked about her new job ____8____ the way to London and before long I **realized**[06] that she was going to work for my firm. My own secretary had just left, so I must be her new boss. It was only fair to tell her.

"Oh, dear," she said. "What a terrible mistake! I wish I had known."

"Never mind," I said. "At least you'll know when your train's late that mine will be, too."

單字片語補充站

01 **lie** [動] 躺、臥（lain 為過去分詞）　**04** **whistle** [名] 警笛

02 **platform** [名] 月台　**05** **strict** [形] 嚴格的

03 **compartment** [名] 車廂　**06** **realize** [動] 了解到、明白

Quiz

( ) **01.** (A) the train to start　(B) for the train start
　　　 (C) the train's start　(D) for the train to start

( ) **02.** (A) on their hour (B) on time (C) at their hour (D) at time

( ) **03.** (A) at place (B) on duty (C) for control (D) in post

( ) **04.** (A) haven't I (B) don't I (C) wasn't I (D) didn't I

( ) **05.** (A) drive to the engine　(B) engine's driver
　　　 (C) conductor's driver　(D) engine driver

( ) **06.** (A) very slower than　(B) much slower than
　　　 (C) a lot more slower than (D) a great deal more slower than

( ) **07.** (A) I'm going to work for　(B) what I'm going to work for
　　　 (C) I'm going to work (D) whom I'm going to work

( ) **08.** (A) through (B) by (C) in (D) on

Two years ago I paid my first visit to a **temple**[01]. My brother was about to take the **Joint College Entrance Examination**[02], and ____1____. I had at first been **reluctant**[03] to go, but ____2____.

It was an interesting **experience**[04] for me, though a pretty ordinary one for my grandmother. I followed her as ____3____. Instead of feeling bored by the **activities**[05], ____4____. As it turned out, ____5____. I don't know, however, whether the **efforts**[06] of my mother and grandmother **contributed**[07] to his **success**[08], or whether he can **take all the credit himself**[09].

單字片語補充站

01 temple [名] 寺廟

02 Joint College Entrance Examination [名] 大學聯考

03 reluctant [形] 不情願的、勉強的

04 experience [名] 經驗

05 activity [名] 活動

06 effort [名] 努力

07 contribute [動] 貢獻

08 success [名] 成功

09 take all the credit himself [片] 歸功於自己

Quiz

(A) my grandmother insisted, and anyway, my curiosity finally got the better of me

(B) my brother did very well on the exam and got a place at the university he wanted

(C) she made all the necessary preparations and went through a variety of rituals and private ceremonies

(D) I accompanied my mother and grandmother to a small temple in our neighborhood to make an offering and pray for his success

(E) I found the whole affair quite fascinating

Unit 26-1: 文章概要及重點理解

　　我家有五個成員。我排行老大,有兩個弟弟。我爸爸是一個非常熱衷工作的公務員。我媽媽是家庭主婦兼好廚師。她非常欣賞中國書法。我的一個弟弟比我小三歲,但是他在知識和智慧方面卻勝過我。我另外一個弟弟只有十二歲。至於我,我的嗜好是集郵和聽古典音樂。

　　每逢週末,我的家人經常聚在一起從事一些活動,例如野餐或舉行宴會。然而,這個週末將會很特別,因為我們要招待四個親戚,包括舅舅、舅媽及二個表兄弟。父親清洗窗戶,並把屋頂漆成綠色。母親洗碗、舖床。弟弟澆花,我掃地。雖然我們都很累,但我們非常快樂。我的表兄弟會和我一起打線上遊戲,我希望他們快點到來。

（A）1. 下列哪一項是作者的嗜好?
　　　A. 聽音樂
　　　B. 製作印章
　　　C. 閱讀經典文學
　　　D. 看電視節目

（C）2. 週末時,作者一家人通常會做什麼?
　　　A. 待在家裡
　　　B. 去看電影
　　　C. 舉辦派對
　　　D. 拜訪祖父母

Unit 26-2: 透過克漏字題型強化文法概念

　　我一個人坐在我常坐的火車小客房中至少有十分鐘了,要等著這班火車開走。從 Littlebury開出的火車從來未曾準時開車,因而我常常想在我離家之前,其實還可以在床上多睡一下,或多喝一杯茶。突然我聽見在車廂外的月台上有人在喊叫。有一名年輕的女子正朝著火車車廂跑過來。那位值班的男士伸出手企圖阻止她,但她還是從他前面通過,上了車廂,打開我客房的門;當時汽笛響了,火車開動了。

　　「我差點就趕不上了，可不是嗎？」那名女子說。「到倫敦要花多久的時間啊？」

　　「那得看火車司機的情形了。」我回答道。「有些時候，它比其他的火車還慢到。」

　　「我得戴支錶，以免明天又遲到了。」她說。「這是我到一家新公司上班工作的第一天，同事們都說我的上司很嚴格。我還沒見到他，因此我還不知道他長什麼樣，不過他聽起來有一點令人害怕。」

　　在到倫敦的途中，她討論著她的新工作，不久我明白她是為我的公司工作。我的秘書剛剛離職，八成我就是她的新老闆吧！把事實告訴她是公平的。

　　「我的天啊！」她說。「多可怕的錯誤啊！但願我早知道就好了。」

　　「沒關係啦，」我說。「至少妳知道，以後當妳的火車慢來時，我的也同樣遲到了。」

1.D　2.B　3.B　4.D　5.D　6.B　7.A　8.D

Unit **26-3: 熟悉篇章的前後銜接關係**

　　兩年前我第一次進到廟裡。那時正逢我弟弟要參加大學聯考，(D)**我陪著媽媽及奶奶到臨近的小廟裡拜拜並祈禱弟弟能順利成功。**起初，我是極不願意與他們前去，(A)**但由於奶奶的堅持，而且不管怎麼樣我的好奇心還是戰勝了我自己！**

　　對我而言，這次還算是滿有趣的經驗，雖然對奶奶來說是再稀鬆平常也不過的事。我跟著她，看(C)**她作大大小小的準備，再經過一堆儀式及私下的祭祀。**(E)**我發覺整個拜拜儀式很令人著迷，一點也不會乏味。**結果，(B)**我弟弟在考場上表現不俗，也如願考上他理想的學校。**然而，我卻不敢斷言弟弟的成功是否是由於媽媽與奶奶的「努力」，還是他自己的功勞。

1.D　2.A　3.C　4.E　5.B

Unit 03-1: 文章概要及重點理解

閱讀全文，並回答下列的問題

Clothing is necessary in our daily lives because it provides us with warmth, privacy, and beauty. In modern times, clothing not only becomes the criteria to judge a person, but also a way of expressing oneself at the same time. Some people are fond of wearing name-brand clothes, and they spend a lot of money on them. However, many teenagers buy these expensive goods at any cost, which causes many social problems. Actually, it doesn't matter whether it's a famous brand or not as long as you wear the clothes that fit your style and age.

Among my clothing, I like the winter coat most. One year ago, my mother sent it to me as a birthday gift. Its color is green-yellow, which is my favorite and the most popular color this year. Besides, its material is composed of fifty percent wool and fifty percent acrylic fiber, so it's not only hand wash but also machine wash. Best of all, the coat is warm enough in cold winter and keeps my heart warm as well.

Quiz

( ) 1. **According to the writer, which below is NOT what clothing represents?**
(A) physiological needs
(B) judgment criteria
(C) expression of oneself
(D) social class

( ) 2. **What does the writer imply when it comes to buying name-brand clothes?**
(A) It's not necessary.
(B) It's one of the goals of life.
(C) It's a terrible behavior.
(D) It's a great way to make friends.

According to the conservative estimate, women in the world spend millions of dollars every year on cleansing creams and **lotions**[01] that promise to keep skin healthy and **youthful**[02]. Of course, they are just fighting ____1____ Nature. As people get older, the oil **glands**[03] in their skin produce less oil, and this causes the skin to become drier. Aging skin begins to wrinkle and **sag**[04], and even to develop brown spots or skin **tumors**[05]. This process is **accelerated**[06] by such things as the wind, or by smoking or improper diet.

The most damaging thing for the skin, however, is sunlight. It's strange that some young girls of nowadays consider suntanned skin to be beautiful. They sunbathe in the summer in order to develop a tan. And girls in places with **mild**[07] climates may go to "tanning salons," which ____2____ special lighting equipment that provides people with artificial suntans. Such prolonged **exposure**[08] to both real and artificial sunlight can ____3____ lead to skin cancer. The answer ____4____ healthy skin is actually the same answer to a healthy body: eat ____5____, exercise ____6____, and ____7____ bad habits such as smoking and drinking.

單字片語補充站

01 **lotion** [名] 乳液

02 **youthful** [形] 年輕的

03 **gland** [名] 腺體

04 **sag** [動] 下陷、下垂

05 **tumor** [名] 腫瘤

06 **accelerate** [動] 加速

07 **mild** [形] 溫和的、適中的

08 **exposure** [名] 暴露

Quiz

( ) **01.** (A) for　　(B) against　　(C) upon　　(D) over

( ) **02.** (A) are equipped with　(B) equips
　　　　(C) are equipping　　　(D) equips with

( ) **03.** (A) lately　(B) hardly　　(C) eventually　(D) merely

( ) **04.** (A) of　　(B) for　　(C) to　　(D) by

( ) **05.** (A) quickly　(B) slowly　　(C) properly　(D) usually

( ) **06.** (A) usually　(B) frequently　(C) regularly　(D) finally

( ) **07.** (A) avoid　(B) create　　(C) enjoy　　(D) throw

Physical beauty is certainly a gift. Many people **strive**[01] to enhance their outer beauty. ____1____ However, some say the **aesthetic**[02] medicine is not necessarily the only path to beauty. ____2____ There is a strong connection between beauty and the way we breathe, our **mindset**[03], and our lifestyle. Our skin **reveals**[04] the emotions and health conditions. For example, when we are going through difficult times, the **complexion**[05] can appear as if aged overnight. ____3____ On the contrary, a balanced mental state and inner **tranquility**[06] makes you **radiate**[07] with beauty from within.

When you can achiever the body-mind-spirit wellness, you will look gorgeous. How can such balanced state be achieved? ____4____ Regular yoga practice helps to put a **refreshing**[08] smile on your face. Your **presence**[09] can thus **uplift**[10] everyone around. ____5____ That is the perfect state to display both inner beauty and outer beauty.

單字片語補充站

01 strive [動] 努力

02 aesthetic [形] 美學的

03 mindset [名] 心態、思想、思維方式

04 reveal [動] 顯示

05 complexion [名] 氣色

06 tranquility [名] 寧靜

07 radiate [動] 發光

08 refreshing [形] 甜美、令人耳目一新

09 presence [名] 出現

10 uplift [動] 使……振奮

 Quiz

(A) Scientific studies have proven that outer beauty is a reflection of inner beauty.

(B) When you have the vitality, your eyes, your expressions, and your attitude can be attractive to others.

(C) Some people develop acnes when they have troubles.

(D) Yoga and meditation are often considered the doorway to the salon beautifying the inner self.

(E) They wear cosmetics or undertake plastic surgeries.

Unit 27-1: 文章概要及重點理解

衣著在我們的生活中是必要的，因為它提供給我們溫暖、隱私、美觀。在現代，服裝不僅成為判斷一個人的指標，同時也是表現自我的一種方法。有些人喜歡穿名牌的衣服，在其中花了很多錢。然而，很多青少年不計代價買那些昂貴的商品，造成許多社會問題。事實上，只要你穿適合自己風格年齡的衣服，是不是名牌並不重要。

在我所有的衣物中，我最喜歡那件冬天的大衣。一年前，我母親把它當生日禮物送給了我。它的顏色是帶綠的黃色，是我最喜歡而且是今年最流行的顏色。此外，它的質料是由**50%** 羊毛及**50%**壓克力人造纖維所組成，所以它不僅可以乾洗也可以用機器洗。最好的是，這件大衣在寒冬時夠溫暖而且也使我的心感到溫暖。

(D) 1. 根據作者，下列何者並非衣裝所代表的？
   A. 生理需求
   B. 判別標準
   C. 自我表達
   D. 社會地位

(A) 2. 對於購買名牌衣服，作者暗示了什麼？
   A. 很不必要。
   B. 是人生目標之一。
   C. 是很糟糕的行為。
   D. 是結交好友的好方法。

Unit 27-2: 透過克漏字題型強化文法概念

根據保守估計，世界上的女性每年花數百萬的錢在清潔乳霜上，只為了使肌膚保持健康與年輕。當然，她們只是在和自然對抗。當人們變老，皮膚裡的油腺產生較少的油脂，皮膚就會變得乾燥。老化的皮膚開始產生皺紋和下垂，甚至長出褐色的斑點或皮膚腫瘤。而風吹、抽煙或不適當的飲食會加速這樣的過程。

然而，陽光對皮膚最具傷害。奇怪的是，有些現代的年輕女性認為曬黑的皮膚是美麗的。她們在夏天做日光浴只為了擁有一身的古銅色。而在溫帶地區的女性，她們可能會去備有特別的照明設備，提供人工日曬用的「曬膚中心」。這樣長時間暴露在真正的日照和人工日照最後會導致皮膚癌。實際上，擁有健康皮膚的答案和擁有健康身體的答案是相同的：正確地飲食、運動，避免像抽煙和喝酒的壞習慣。

1.B　2.A　3.C　4.C　5.C　6.C　7.C　8.A

Unit 27-3: 熟悉篇章的前後銜接關係

外表的美麗毫無疑問是得天獨厚的條件。許多人努力要讓外表美麗。**(E) 他們使用化妝品或者去做整形手術。**但是，有些人說醫美並不是唯一達到美麗的途徑。**(A) 科學研究證明外表的美麗其實是內在美的反映。**美麗和我們呼吸的方式、我們的思考模式、以及我們的生活方式密切相關。我們的皮膚顯示出我們的情緒和健康狀況。例如，當我們經歷難關時，臉色就會好像一夜之間變老一樣。**(C) 有些人甚至還會在有煩惱的時候長出青春痘。**相反地，平衡的心理狀態以及內在的平靜，會讓你因內在美而容光煥發。

當你可以達到身心靈的健康狀態，就會看起來狀態極佳。要如何達到這種均衡的狀態呢？**(D) 瑜伽和沈思常常被認為是美化內在自我的入門方式。**固定練習瑜伽可以讓你神清氣爽、常保持微笑。你一出現就鼓舞了周圍的人。**(B) 當你展現活力，你的眼神、表情、和態度就會很迷人。**這就是展現出內在美和外在美的絕佳狀態。

1.E　2.A　3.C　4.D　5.B

Unit 28-1: 文章概要及重點理解

閱讀全文，並回答下列的問題

I wonder how often your family has bought new furniture, curtains or kitchen equipment and then wondered how to dispose of the old items that still have quite a lot of life left in them.

It was in response to this situation that The Carpenters' Shop was opened in the town of Walsall, England. Run by a team of church volunteers, the shop will collect any surplus, good-quality items and store them until they can be redistributed to the people who are in need of those particular things.

Many have been helped through the scheme, including single parents, disabled people and the elderly, and those who have lost all their household possessions through a disaster such as a house fire.

It's an admirable project, and it is worth finding out if a similar one operates in your hometown. Participation costs the donor nothing and can make such a difference to others.

( ) 1. **The phrase "dispose of" in the first paragraph can best be replaced by _____.**
(A) put up with
(B) get rid of
(C) look down upon
(D) take notice of

( ) 2. **The purpose of setting up The Carpenters' Shop was _____.**
(A) to help those who could not afford certain household items
(B) to open a furniture store run by church volunteers
(C) to teach people how to destroy disposable furniture
(D) to sell good-quality furniture to disabled people

( ) 3. **What is the author's opinion of an item that someone doesn't need any longer?**
(A) It's normally out of style.
(B) It should be donated to charity.
(C) It's an admirable project.
(D) There may be something wrong with it.

Plastic **utensils**[01] and **disposable**[02] containers may have brought convenience to people's daily life, ____1____ the discarded items have brought greater **hazard**[03] to the natural environment. ____2____ a large amount of garbage could be **incinerated**[04], a ____3____ of garbage ended up in the ocean. A collection of plastic and floating trash has formed the Great Pacific Garbage Patch, ____4____ is located in the ocean between Hawaii and California. The masses of marine **debris**[05] particles ____5____ from the Pacific Rim, including countries in Asia, North America, and South America. The garbage patch is also known as the Pacific trash **vortex**[06]. It has ____6____ high concentration of plastic, chemical **sludge**[07], wood pulp, and other debris caught in the current. Items like plastic lighters, toothbrushes, water bottles, pens, cell phones, and plastic bags could be found in the patch.

Though in the commonly public **perception**[08], the patch ____7____ as giant island of floating rubbish, it is not easily detected by the satellite imagery or even casual boaters or divers in the area. The patch is ____8____ of dispersed fingernail-sized or smaller bits of plastic. ____9____ the Ocean Cleanup project, the patch covers 1.6 million square kilometers. Also, based on the **estimation**[09] of United Nations Environmental Program, there are about "46000 pieces of plastic for every square mile of ocean." The concentration that increases **exponentially**[10] may ____10___ immeasurable damage to the marine environment around the globe, which may eventually have impact on human food chain, economy, and society.

單字片語補充站

01 **utensil** [名] 器具

02 **disposable** [形] 用過即丟的

03 **hazard** [名] 危害

04 **incinerate** [動] 焚化

05 **debris** [名] 碎屑

06 **vortex** [名] 渦流

07 **sludge** [名] 污泥

08 **perception** [名] 認知

09 **estimation** [名] 估計

10 **exponentially** [副] 指數地

Quiz

( ) **01.** (A) and   (B) or   (C) but   (D) so

( ) **02.** (A) Because (B) While (C) Since (D) Despite

( ) **03.** (A) grip (B) gear (C) gust (D) gyre

( ) **04.** (A) which (B) that (C) what (D) where

( ) **05.** (A) excluded   (B) deviated   (C) results   (D) originate

( ) **06.** (A) extraordinarily   (B) exceptionally
      (C) exclusively   (D) experimentally

( ) **07.** (A) exists   (B) existing   (C) to exist   (D) have existed

( ) **08.** (A) included   (B) made up   (C) consisted (D) composed

( ) **09.** (A) On account that   (B) Instead of
      (C) According to   (D) Compared with

( ) **10.** (A) cause (B) lead   (C) bring   (D) lead

____1____, the amount of garbage in Taiwan increased **enormously**[01]. It is getting more and more difficult to deal with the garbage problem. Our government used to throw the garbage in the dump. However, today it is almost impossible to find a piece of land for garbage **disposal**[02]. ____2____, the local **residents**[03] will **protest against**[04] it. It is because no one is willing to live near a dump site or an **incinerator**[05].

In fact, ____3____. It is time for every one of us to do something to protect our environment. ____4____. In order to **alleviate**[06] this problem, ____5____. If everybody does his best to protect our environment from further **degradation**[07], this problem is sure to be solved.

單字片語補充站

01 **enormously** [副] 非常

02 **disposal** [名] 清除、拋棄

03 **resident** [名] 居民

04 **protest against** [片] 抗議、反對

05 **incinerator** [名] 焚化爐

06 **alleviate** [動] 減輕、舒緩

07 **degradation** [名] 危害

Quiz

(A) it is not only our government's but also everybody's responsibility to deal with the garbage problem

(B) We must show our concern for the disposal of garbage

(C) With the rapid growth of population

(D) we should reduce as much garbage as possible and recycle garbage in our daily life

(E) Whenever a new dump site is going to be set up

Unit 28-1: 文章概要及重點理解

我不知道你家多久買一次新家具、窗簾、或廚房用具，然後不知如何處理掉那些仍可以使用頗久的舊物件。

為了因應這種情況，「木匠商店」在英國史達弗郡的華索鎮開設了。由一群教會義工所經營，這家商店收集任何多餘而品質良好的物件，並將其儲藏到它們能重新分配給那些有特別需要的人為止。

經由此計劃已有許多人受到了幫助，包括單親父母、殘障人士、老人，以及那些因為火災之類的災禍而失去所有家當的人。

這個計劃令人敬佩，因此值得去瞭解是否有相似的計畫在你的家鄉運作。參與此工作計畫對捐贈者不費分文，但卻可以對別人產生極大的影響。

(B) 1. 第一段中的詞組「dispose of」可以 用什麼詞組來代替？
　　A. 忍受　　　　　　　　B. **擺脫、丟棄**
　　C. 輕視　　　　　　　　D. 注意到

(A) 2. 設立「木匠的店」的目的是什麼？
　　A. **幫助那些不能負擔特定家具費用的人**
　　B. 開一家由教會志工經營的家具店
　　C. 教人們怎麼摧毀拋棄性家具
　　D. 賣高品質的家具給身心障礙人士

(B) 3. 作者對於不再需要的家具有什麼看法？
　　A. 它通常很過時　　　　　B. **它應該被捐到慈善機構**
　　C. 它是個很值得讚美的計畫　D. 它可能有什麼問題

Unit 28-2: 透過克漏字題型強化文法概念

塑膠器具以及一次性的容器可能有為人類日常生活帶來便利，但是丟棄的物品對於自然環境帶來了更大的危害。雖然有大量的垃圾可以被焚化，還是有很多垃圾最後落在海洋的迴旋中。大量的塑膠和漂浮的垃圾形成了太平洋垃圾帶，位在夏威夷和加州之間的海洋中。海中大量的碎屑粒子是來自環太平洋帶，包括亞洲、北美、和南美的國家。太平洋垃圾袋又稱為太平洋垃圾渦流。它集中特別大量的塑膠、化學污泥、木漿、以及其他落在洋流中的碎屑。這個垃圾帶當中還可以發現塑膠打火機、牙刷、水瓶、筆、手機、以及塑膠袋等物品。

雖然一般人會認為太平洋垃圾帶就是一大塊漂浮的垃圾島，但是衛星很難擷取它的影像，偶然經過這一區的小船或潛水者也不太會發現它的存在。這個垃圾帶是由分散的、指甲大小的塑膠粒組成的。根據海洋清理基金會的說法，這個垃圾帶涵蓋了160萬平方公里的面積。此外，聯合國環境規劃署的估計顯示，有大約「每平方英里的海洋中會有4萬6千的塑膠碎片。」以指數型速率成長的垃圾集中量可能會對全球的海洋環境造成無法估計的損害，最後會衝擊到人類的食物鏈、經濟、及社會層面。

1.C　2.B　3.D　4.A　5.D　6.B　7.A　8.D　9.C　10.A

Unit **28-3**: 熟悉篇章的前後銜接關係

(C)隨著人口的迅速增長，台灣的垃圾量大量增加。處理垃圾問題變得愈來愈困難。我們的政府過去總是把垃圾傾倒在垃圾處理場。可是現在幾乎不可能找到一塊地方來棄置垃圾。(E)每當一座新的掩埋場準備要設立的時候，當地的居民就會反對。這是因為沒有人願意住在垃圾場或是焚化爐的旁邊。

其實，(A)處理垃圾問題不只是政府的責任，也是每一個人的責任。現在該是我們每一個人採取行動來保護我們環境的時候了。(B)我們必須對丟棄垃圾問題表示關心。為了紓解這個問題，(D)我們應該盡可能減少垃圾的數量，並且每天做垃圾回收的工作。如果每一個人都能盡力保護我們的環境以免變得更糟，問題一定可以解決。

1.C　2.E　3.A　4.B　5.D

Unit 29 Hobbies and Entertainments
興趣娛樂篇

Unit 29-1: 文章概要及重點理解
閱讀全文，並回答下列的問題

Taipei is a city of many faces, where you can experience a typical urban lifestyle and understand the traditional aspect of Chinese culture. In addition to all the high-rise office towers, there are still some amazing Greens, such as Ta-An Forest Park, Taipei Botanical Garden and Yangmingshan National Park. As the capital of ROC, Taipei is the political, financial and fashion center of the island. Taipei 101, still the world's top ten building so far, has become a new landmark of Taipei, attracting thousands of people who want to keep up with the latest fashion and follow a fashionable lifestyle. The Eslite Bookstore, which stays open for 24 hours, is a paradise for booklovers and night owls. Due to the excellent public transportation system, including the MRT and buses, it is very easy to get around in Taipei.

Taichung is a paradise for both shoppers and people who enjoy a relaxed / cozy atmosphere. For shoppers, there are not only huge department stores but also many European-style boutique stores in Taichung. After a long day of shopping, people can take a rest in spacious cafes or in teahouses located in traditional Chinese gardens. While most people in Taiwan focus their attention to the competition between Taipei and Kaohsiung, it is often forgotten that Taichung has the potential to be an international metropolis.

Quiz

( ) 1. **According to the article, you CANNOT find which one below in Taipei?**
(A) Chinese traditional culture
(B) modern tall buildings
(C) green plants
(D) wide crop fields

( ) 2. **Which city in Taiwan has been seen as a shopping paradise?**
(A) Taipei
(B) Tainan
(C) Taichung
(D) Taitung

The **charm**[01] of sports is watching **athletes**[02] test the very **boundaries**[03] of human ability. Adidas' **slogan**[04] "Impossible is nothing" **conveys**[05] ____1____ feeling well. The commercials ____2____ showed superhuman sport skills are simply exciting to watch. ____3____ a sports lover, of the numerous kinds of sports, I like badminton the most. First, playing badminton helps ____4____ to stay fit but lose weight. **Furthermore**[06], badminton is easy to learn and we don't need large space to play it.

Every Sunday morning is the happiest time, when my family regularly **gathers**[07] together, playing badminton. My parents, both busy ____5____ during the weekdays, can get exercise and sweat off some weight. And my sister and I can **relieve**[08] some pressure from heavy schoolwork. ____6____ playing badminton, one needs to work with the partner to win the game, which brings together our family. What's more, we tend to go to the coffee shop after playing badminton. Then we can share what happened in life in the past week. With so many benefits, no wonder I think of playing badminton my lifelong interest.

單字片語補充站

01 **charm** [名] 魅力

02 **athlete** [名] 運動員

03 **boundary** [名] 界線、極限

04 **slogan** [名] 標語

05 **convey** [動] 傳達

06 **furthermore** [副] 此外

07 **gather** [動] 聚集、聚會

08 **relieve** [動] 紓解

 Quiz

( ) **01.** (A) one (B) that (C) which (D) at

( ) **02.** (A) themselves (B) they (C) those (D) these

( ) **03.** (A) For (B) As (C) By (D) From

( ) **04.** (A) not (B) not only (C) just (D) still

( ) **05.** (A) work (B) to work (C) working (D) at work

( ) **06.** (A) To (B) By (C) With (D) While

As Otaku culture thrives, there is a new trend in the **entertainment**[01] industry – virtual **hologram**[02] singer. ____1____ The **intriguing**[03] virtual **celebrities**[04] have turned the trend into a billion-dollar market. ____2____ With her worldwide **popularity**[05], tickets to her concerts are often sold out within a few days. On the other hand, Tianyui had her first concert **accompanied**[06] by world-renowned Chinese pianist Lang Lang in March 4th , 2019. ____3____ This unusual show is reported to be the result of six months of hard work by **roughly**[07] 200 production **staff**[08].

____4____ It's different from the holograms of Michael Jackson 'performed' on stage in the past decade. ____5____ The **motion capture**[09], 3D modeling, and a backstage **voice dubber** [10] made it possible for her to have real-time interaction with Lang Lang during the concert. To Tianyi's fans, her charm is no less than a human popular music artist.

單字片語補充站

01 entertainment [名] 娛樂

02 hologram [名] 全息投影

03 intriguing [形] 有趣的、引人入勝的、神祕的

04 celebrity [名] 名人

05 popularity [名] 人氣

06 accompany [動] 陪伴、伴奏

07 roughly [副] 大約

08 staff [名] 工作人員

09 motion capture [名] 動作捕捉

10 voice dubber [名] 配音員

 Quiz

(A) Hastune has accumulated 2.5 million followers on social media since her debut in 2009.

(B) Virtual idols like Hatsune Miku in Japan and Luo Tianyi in China have been created.

(C) Tianyi's voice and personality are created with sophisticated technology.

(D) The holographic performance of Tianyi is not based on a particular human performer.

(E) Thousands of fans convened at Shanghai's Mercedes-Benz arena for Tanyi's performance.

Unit **29-1:** 文章概要及重點理解

台北是個多面的城市,在這裡你能體會典型的都會生活,也能瞭解中國文化中傳統的一面。除了高樓大廈之外,台北還有令人驚奇的多處綠地,像是大安森林公園、台北植物園還有陽明山國家公園。身為中華民國的首都,台北同時是政治、金融和流行的中心。「台北一〇一」目前是世界上前十高的大樓,它已成為台北的新地標,吸引了成千上萬想要跟上最新時尚、體驗流行生活的人來到此地。二十四小時營業的誠品書店,是愛書人和夜貓族的天堂。有了由捷運和公車所形成的優良大眾運輸系統,在台北趴趴走一點也不難。

台中對於血拼族及喜愛享受輕鬆氣氛的人是個購物的天堂。對血拼族而言,台中不但有很大的百貨公司,也有很多歐式精品店。在一天的採購之後,人們可以在寬敞的咖啡館或是座落於中式古典花園中的茶樓中小憩。台灣人大都注意台北和高雄之間的競爭,卻常忘了台中其實也同樣具有發展為國際大都會的潛力。

(D) 1. 根據短文,你不能在台北找到什麼?
　　　A. 中華傳統文化
　　　B. 現代高聳大樓
　　　C. 綠色植物
　　　D. 廣大作物農田

(C) 2 台灣的哪一個城市被視為購物天堂?
　　　A. 台北
　　　B. 台南
　　　C. 台中
　　　D. 台東

Unit 29-2: 透過克漏字題型強化文法概念

　　運動的魅力在於看著運動家挑戰人類能力的極限。艾迪達的口號「『不可能』不算什麼」很恰當地傳達了這個感覺。它的廣告裡面展示著超人的運動技藝，讓人光是看著就感到刺激。我身為一個運動熱愛者，在眾多運動中，我最喜歡的運動是羽球。首先，羽球不只有助於保持健康，還能減肥。再者，羽球學起來容易，也不需用到很大的空間。

　　每個星期天早上是我最快樂的時光，因為我們家人都固定在那天早上聚在一起打羽球。我爸媽，平常都忙於工作，可以活動筋骨還可以流汗減重。而我姐姐跟我可以紓解一些來自繁重課業的壓力。打羽球的時候，必須要跟夥伴合作才能贏得比賽，這可以讓我們家人的感情更親密。更棒的是，我們在打完羽球後常會去喝咖啡。我們會一起分享在過去一個 禮拜發生的大小事情。有這麼多的好處，難怪我認為打羽球是我終生的興趣。

1.B　2.A　3.B　4.B　5.D　6.D

Unit 29-3: 熟悉篇章的前後銜接關係

　　宅文化的興盛帶動了娛樂產業中一個新的趨勢——虛擬的全息投影歌手。**(B) 像日本的初音和中國的洛天依這類虛擬偶像已經被創造出來了。**這些有趣又神秘的虛擬名人將這個趨勢轉變成十億元的市場。**(A) 自從2009年出道以來，初音已經在社群網站累積250萬粉絲。**因為她在全球的知名度，她演唱會的票總是在幾天之內就賣完。另一方面，天依在2019年3月4日與世界知名的中國鋼琴家郎朗同台，開了首場演唱會。**(E) 數千名粉絲聚集在上海的賓士廣場來看天依的表演。**據報導，這個特別的表演是大約兩百位製作團隊成員努力六個月才有的成果。

　　(D) 天依的全息投影表演不是以一個人類表演者為範本。它和過去十年麥可傑克森的全息投影在舞台上「表演」的方式不一樣。**(C) 天依的聲音和人格是以精密科技發展出來的。**動作捕捉技術、3D模型、以及後台的配音人員讓天依可以在演唱會上與郎朗即時互動。對天依的樂迷來說，她的魅力是不輸給人類流行歌手的。

1.B　2.A　3.E　4.D　5.C

Mobile Communication
手機通訊篇

Unit 30-1: 文章概要及重點理解
閱讀全文，並回答下列的問題

New laws concerning cell phone use while driving a car or riding a motorcycle are going to be implemented. Beginning in September, those who use cell phones while driving will be fined from NT$ 1,000 to NT$ 3,000. Transportation authorities have called on people to install a hands-free phone kit if they want to make phone calls while behind the wheel. Police will stop cars and motorcycles if drivers are found violating the regulations or take pictures of them in the act if stopping the vehicle would affect the flow of traffic.

Whether talking on a phone increases the risk of an accident has long been a controversial issue. Those who maintain drivers should be allowed to use mobile phones argue that a phone could be a lifesaver in an emergency, such as when someone needs emergency medical treatment. That argument is to a large extent valid. A mobile phone can be a valuable tool for a driver. It is also time-saving because the driver can complete a job while driving. But mobile phones are known to have been the cause of many traffic accidents. Research suggests that using a cell phone makes driving riskier. A study indicates that using a cell phone increases the chance of a traffic accident by 38 percent. The reason is, according to the study, that cell phone use makes the driver less alert to hazards on the road and slower in applying the brakes. To make the new regulations a success, it is necessary to give car owners a clear picture of the connection between cell phone use and traffic accidents. We hope the policy will be successfully implemented.

( ) 1. **Which of the following is a disadvantage of using a cellphone?**
   (A) It helps a lot when there is an emergency.
   (B) A driver may talk business while driving.
   (C) A husband caught in a traffic jam can call home to inform his wife that he will be late.
   (D) It makes drivers less sensitive to the conditions of the road.

( ) 2. **Which of the following statements is true?**
   (A) Drivers caught using a cellphone while driving will be fined.
   (B) On no account will drivers talk on the phone while driving.
   (C) Drivers using a cellphone while driving will definitely be stopped and given a ticket.
   (D) Everyone agrees that talking on the phone and driving at the same time is highly dangerous.

The smartphone has brought a lot of **convenience**[01] to our daily life. ____1____, as we become more reliant ____2____ the mobile **gadget**[02] in our daily **routines**[03] for communication or even financing procedures, we should raise the awareness about the mobile security. ____3____ threats keep evolving and **adjusting**[04] based on new kinds of platforms and services, we might be the target of viruses and **cyber-attacks**[05] at some point or ____4____. Below are some tips that can help you **navigate**[06] your mobile device in a secure way.

One of the **fundamentals**[07] is to keep your device ____5____ with a passcode, a pattern, fingerprint, or face recognition. Also, be sure to set the shortest time for automatically ____6____ the lock. This can at least prevent the thief form **accessing**[08] your complete personal information immediately from your stolen device. ____7____ to secure Wifi is also rather basic for every mobile gadget user. Choosing a virtual private network or VPN when using public Wifi can keep your information ____8____ prying eyes. Finally, it would be ____9____ to **encrypt**[09] the data on your cellphone so that the emails, contacts, and financial information may be at lower risk ____10____ the **device**[10] get stolen. The encryption process can be enacted by choosing the "Encrypt Phone" in the settings menu on your phone.

單字片語補充站

01 convenience [名] 便利

02 gadget [名] 小工具

03 routine [名] 規律

04 adjust [動] 調整

05 cyber-attack [名] 網路攻擊

06 navigate [動] 操作

07 fundamental [形] 基礎

08 access [動] 取得

09 encrypt [動] 加密

10 device [名] 裝置

Quiz

( ) **01.** (A) Fortunately (B) Otherwise
(C) Additionally (D) However

( ) **02.** (A) in (B) on (C) by (D) for

( ) **03.** (A) Since (B)Without (C) As (D) Despite

( ) **04.** (A) the other (B) others (C) another (D) other

( ) **05.** (A) locked (B) lacked (C) lashed (D) leaked

( ) **06.** (A) enacts (B) enacting (C) enacted (D) to enact

( ) **07.** (A) Connecting (B) Communicating
(C) Contacting (D) Commuting

( ) **08.** (A) to (B) by (C) from (D) under

( ) **09.** (A) doubtful (B) helpful (C) hopeful (D) mournful

( ) **10.** (A) would (B) might (C) could (D) should

_____1_____ It enables touches to be sensed through a protective layer in front of a **display**[01]. _____2_____ The complete system resists impacts, scratches, and vandalism. It is also unaffected by moisture, heat, rain, snow and ice, or harsh cleaning fluids, making it ideal for outdoor applications. _____3_____ Therefore, the projected capacitivity technology is widely applied everywhere on outdoor kiosks, ticketing machines, ATMs, web phones, pay-at-the pump gas machines, and of course, iPhone.

iPhone is equipped with projective **capacitive**[02] technology instead of **resistive**[03] touch technology, a technology which is most commonly used so far. _____4_____ Such screens already detect the **proximity**[04] of a finger from 2 millimeters away. With so many benefits, **shipments**[05] of this advanced strain of touch screens are projected to jump from fewer than 200,000 units in 2006 to more than 21 million units by 2012, with the bulk of the **components**[06] going to mobile phones, according to a forecast by iSuppli Corp., a **research**[07] company. Francis Lee, chief executive of Synaptics Inc., a maker of touch sensors even **predicted**[08] that _____5_____.

單字片語補充站

01 display [名] 顯示、顯像

02 capacitive [形] 電容的

03 resistive [形] 電阻的

04 proximity [名] 接近、親近

05 shipment [名] 出貨

06 component [名] 零件

07 research [名] 研究

08 predict [動] 預測

 **Quiz**

(A) In other words, it allows touch monitors to be installed behind store windows or vandal-resistant glass.

(B) This new user interface will be like a tsunami, hitting an entire spectrum of devices.

(C) That's why iPhone's capacitive sensors don't even need actual physical contact.

(D) Projected capacitive is a kind of touch screen sensor technology.

(E) What's more, you can use the touch screen when wearing gloves.

Unit 30-1: 文章概要及重點理解

有關開車或騎摩托車時使用行動電話的新法規即將實施。從九月份開始，開車時講行動電話的人將處以新台幣一千元至三千元的罰金。交通部呼籲大眾如果想在開車時打電話，就要安裝免持聽筒的電話裝置。駕駛人違規時，警方將會攔下汽車或機車，攔車會影響車流的話，就當場照像舉證。

長久以來開車時講電話是否會增加危險發生意外的可能性一直是爭議性的議題。主張駕駛人應被允許使用行動電話的人認為情況緊急時，它可能會是個救命恩人，例如當某人需要緊急醫療時。這種論點相當有道理。行動電話對駕駛人而言，可能是很重要的工具。它能節省時間，因為駕駛人開車時就可辦完事。然而大家都知道行動電話是許多車禍的原因。研究指出開車時使用行動電話會使開車更具危險性。有項研究顯示，開車時使用行動電話會使發生車禍的可能性增加百分之三十八。根據這項研究，其原因是開車時使用行動電話會使駕駛人對於路上危險的警覺性降低，踩煞車的反應也會變慢。

為了新法規的成功施行，讓車主清楚地了解開車時使用行動電話和交通事故間的關聯性是有必要的。我們期望這個新政策能圓滿實行。

(D) 1. 以下何者是使用行動電話的缺點？
A. 有緊急情況時，它助益良多。
B. 開車時，駕駛人可以談生意。
C. 因在塞車中的丈夫可告知他的太太會晚點回家。
D. 它使駕駛人對路上狀況的警覺性降低。

(A) 2. 以下敘述何者為真？
A. 被逮到在開車時講行動電話的駕駛人將被處以罰金。
B. 駕駛人絕不能在開車時講電話。
C. 駕駛人開車時使用行動電話一定會攔下並被開罰單。
D. 每個人都認同一邊講電話一邊開車危險性是很高的。

Unit 30-2: 透過克漏字題型強化文法概念

　　智慧型手機為我們的日常生活帶來許多便利。但是，當我們更加依賴手機來進行溝通或者處理財務時，應該要更加注意手機通訊的安全性。手機威脅隨著新型的平台和服務出現而不斷地調整和進化，而我們也隨時有可能成為病毒和網路攻擊的目標。以下有一些小技巧，可以幫助你在安全地使用手機。

　　其中一個基本的方式是要用密碼、解鎖圖形、或臉部辨識來鎖住手機。此外，注意把自動鎖住手機的時間設成最短。這樣至少可以防止小偷立刻就能從你被竊取的手機中取得你完整的個人資訊。連接到安全的網路也是每個行動裝置使用者應該要注意的基本原則。要使用公開無線網路的時候，選擇一個隱密的網域或者虛擬私人網路可以防止你的個人資料被竊取。最後，萬一你的手機失竊了，手機資訊加密可以降低你的電子郵件、通訊錄、金融資訊等被竊的風險。資料加密的過程可以透過你手機設定選單上面的「手機加密」選項開始執行。

1.D　2.B　3.C　4.C　5.A　6.B　7.A　8.C　9.B　10.D

Unit 30-3: 熟悉篇章的前後銜接關係

　　(D)投射式電容技術是一種觸碰螢幕的感應科技。它可以讓碰觸透過在顯像前的保護層被感應到。(A)換句話說，它可以讓觸碰螢幕者透過商店櫥窗或防暴玻璃下達指令。整個系統可以抵抗撞擊、刮傷和惡意破壞。它也不受潮濕、熱、雨、冰雪或強力清潔劑的影響，用於戶外應用相當理想。(E)還有，當你帶著手套時也可以使用觸控螢幕。因此，投射式電容技術被廣泛應用在戶外書香享、售票機、提款機、網路電話、自助式加油站，還有，iPhone當然也是。

　　iPhone裝置了投射式電容技術，而非迄今為止最常見的電阻式觸碰技術。(C)這也是為什麼iPhone的電容感應器甚至不需要真的物理接觸。在兩毫米遠時螢幕便已偵測到手指的接近。根據一家研究公司iSuppli的報告，有這麼多好處，這種先進品種的觸碰式螢幕出貨計畫從2006年僅20萬個增至2012年時兩千一百萬個，並將伴隨著大量的手機零件出貨。製造觸碰式螢幕的Synaptics公司總裁Francis李甚至預測，(B)新的使用者介面會像海嘯一樣，席捲整個機械設備的光譜。

1.D　2.A　3.E　4.C　5.B

Hi, everyone. My name is James and I live in the city of Toronto. Mine is a harmonious family, which consists of my parents and a brother and a sister. My father is strict with kids, so I have been taught to behave myself and to work hard for my future. I have developed a great interest in music and basketball. My favorite singer is Jay Chou and I hope to be as talented as he is. Of course, in my mind, recreation is as important as studies.

Because I have a penchant for music, I hope that I can spend more time develop my knowledge in different fields of arts during the high school days. In a word, I am very easy to get along with, so I hope to share whatever I know with all my friends. I like to be friends with people with different interests. Thus, I welcome anyone who would like to talk to me or contact me by e-mail.

( ) 1. **According to the article, how can we describe the personality of the writer?**
   (A) easy-going
   (B) out-going
   (C) people person
   (D) absent-minded

( ) 2. **Which one below is NOT one of the writer's self-expectations?**
   (A) To be as talented as his idol.
   (B) To share knowledge with his friends.
   (C) To save money as much as possible.
   (D) To devote himself into different fields of art.

Three years in high school was a string of days filled with bitterness and sweetness. I usually had to get up at six in the morning, going out when it was dark ____1____ be late for the quiz before the flag-raising **ceremony**[01]. After eight long classes, I had no choice ____2____ stay in school to study until nine. The winter was fine, yet when summer came, the nights were hot and **humid**[02] and **accompanied**[03] by mosquitoes and other insects that **distract**[04] me ____3____ my studies. ____4____ the **hardship**[05], those days of **striving**[06] with my classmates toward a common goal, ____5____ needing to worry about other things, were really **fulfilling**[07] and pleasant.

In addition to studying, I still had time to join school clubs. Encouraged by my classmates, I joined the anime **appreciation**[08] club. I looked forward to every meeting of the club because it always cheered me up. I am deeply **convinced**[09] that a student can learn a lot from life in school if he or she takes a positive attitude toward it. Though so much studying is **exhausting**[10], I often remind myself that the purpose of studying is not only to pass exams but also to be well educated. I believe that it will be worth the effort in the end. I will win a place at the college I most want to go to, and I will be on my way to a successful future.

單字片語補充站

01 ceremony [名] 典禮、儀式　　**06 strive** [動] 鬥爭

02 humid [形] 潮濕的　　**07 fulfilling** [形] 滿足的

03 accompany [動] 陪伴、伴隨　　**08 appreciation** [名] 欣賞

04 distract [動] 使分心　　**09 convince** [動] 説服

05 hardship [名] 困境　　**10 exhausting** [形] 疲累的

Quiz

( ) 01. (A) to　　(B) in order to　(C) in order not to　(D) so as to

( ) 02. (A) but to　(B) to　　(C) but　　(D) that

( ) 03. (A) from　(B) to　　(C) when　　(D) by

( ) 04. (A) Despite of　(B) In spite of　(C) Other then　(D) With

( ) 05. (A) and　(B) but　　(C) with　　(D) without

____1____, we can **hardly**[01] see any stars when looking up at the sky. That's why I like to get away from the city sometimes, to find open spaces without any man-made **constructions**[02]. ____2____, I went camping in the mountains with my classmates. At night, we had a lot of fun and games, such as **hide-and-seek**[03], and dancing around the **campfire**[04] that we made / set up.

____3____, and chatted with one another. After midnight, I told my classmates of my **fantasy**[05] of making friends with **aliens**[06]. ____4____. We discussed my crazy idea the whole night and none of us got any sleep. When the sun **rose**[07], ____5____, but it had been a night worth remembering.

單字片語補充站

01 **hardly** [副] 幾乎不

02 **construction** [名] 建築物

03 **hide-and-seek** [名] 捉迷藏

04 **campfire** [名] 營火

05 **fantasy** [名] 幻想

06 **alien** [名] 外星人

07 **rise** [動] 升起

 **Quiz**

(A) When I was a freshman in senior high school

(B) They burst into laughing

(C) Living in a city full of buildings and neon lights

(D) I was tired to death

(E) The best moment was when we looked up at the bright moon and the stars shinning in the sky

Unit **31-1**: 文章概要及重點理解

嗨，大家好，我的名字是James，我住在多倫多市。我的家庭很融洽，包含了我的雙親和一個哥哥、一個姊姊。我父親對孩子很嚴格，因此我一直被教導要循規蹈矩，而要努力奮鬥未來。我對音樂和籃球有很高的興趣。我最喜歡的歌手是周杰倫，而且我希望和他一樣的有才華。當然，在我心目中，娛樂和學業是一樣重要的。

因為我對音樂一直很喜愛，我希望在高中時多花點時間培養對於各藝術領域的知識。總之，我是一個很容易相處的人，所以我希望把我所知道的都分享給我的朋友。我喜歡與具有各種不同興趣的人交朋友。所以我歡迎任何人跟我聊天或用電子郵件跟我聯絡。

(A) 1. 根據短文，我們可以如何形容作者的個性？
　　　A. 好相處
　　　B. 很活潑
　　　C. 受歡迎
　　　D. 心不在焉

(C) 2. 下列敘述何者並非作者的自我期許？
　　　A. 像他的偶像一樣有才華。
　　　B. 和朋友分享知識。
　　　C. 盡可能地省錢。
　　　D. 投身於藝術的各個領域。

Unit **31-2**: 透過克漏字題型強化文法概念

高中這三年是一連串既苦澀又甜美的日子。我常在清晨六點就必須起床，在天色尚暗時出門，以趕上升旗前的小考。上完漫長的八節課後，我還得留在學校自習到九點。在冬天還好，可是一到夏天，晚上悶熱無比，又有大量的蚊蟲，以致讀書常無法專心。雖然辛苦，但不需煩惱其他事情，與同學們一起朝著同一個目標努力的時光，實在是充實又快樂。